T0368683

Remember

Amanda Suddeth

AuthorHouse™
1663 Liberty Drive
Bloomington, IN 47403
www.authorhouse.com
Phone: 1-800-839-8640

First published by AuthorHouse 02/25/2011

ISBN: 978-1-4567-3877-8 (sc)
ISBN: 978-1-4567-3878-5 (e-b)

Library of Congress Control Number: 2011903003

Printed in the United States of America

About The Book

I am who I am because of what I've done, where I've been, and whom I've loved and lost along the way. I am a thinker. I get lost in my mind and find it a great release to write it down, let it go, walk away, and never look back.

I do not live within the conventional. I do not care for rules and guidelines. I rarely follow the traditional poetic outline. Some find it appalling; others love the freedom my writing style gives them when reading. One of my favorite books, *Writing Down the Bones*, has helped shape me, changing me from the writer the teachers all wanted me to be into the writer I always longed to be—and have finally become.

Sweet/Wild/Woman/Child. Within this book of poetry you will find it all: sex, love, hate, pain, revenge, trust, fear, lies, truths, and any number of feelings … spelled out as provocatively as words allow.

A Division of Geologic Chronology

Time is ubiquitous and yet there is no timeline for it.
You cannot define it—
You cannot stop it—
You cannot recreate it—
Time is a handcuff, for which no one has the key,
Always alone and surrounded by people.

Addicted

I am hooked
On the drug
Addicted to you
Rehabilitation
Free me from the fix
Addicted to you

Addiction

My anger and impulsiveness will get the best of me.
I need to free myself from the likes of me.
What is left but the love you try to share with me?
I am stuck, in full-speed addiction, to a drug called you.

What an addiction I feed,
What an addiction I need.
I need to be fed by the drug of you.

Love is the drug that I need;
Love is the drug that I feed;
Love is the drug that kills me;
Love is the addiction—
I love.

Are You Sure

What's up? What are you doing to yourself?
You know you need a lot more healing time.
Why do you allow yourself to get so upset
Over things you only suspect are true?
I love you. Please, shape up.
Learn to love you—
Do it for me.
Be alone. Ignore your feelings of pain;
Believe you are worth it.
I know how you feel. Trust me,
I am your angel.
Why can't that be enough?

All Different Things

Butterfly kisses
Broken wings
Sadness craves
The weirdest things
Eskimo kisses
Frozen grasp
I actually thought
This could last
Soggy kisses
Wet and cold
The numbness is starting
To get old
Kisses sweet
Kisses serene
I've heard them called
Many different things
Kisses stolen
Kisses saved
Give me strength
To walk away

All I Wish: for Him to Walk Away

I am talking to the man I love,
The man who left me,
The man I walked behind.
He is married now;
He knows how I feel,
And yet he calls me
To tell me he loves me still …
How unfair is that to me?

Alone

Alone under satin sheets of blue
In the still of my room, I lie naked
Silence surrounds my beating heart.
I feel you. In the presence of nothingness
I smell your breath, so sweet, so pure;
The curtains from the window dance wildly before my eyes
A distraction to keep my mind from you,
My blue-eyed abandonment. How I wish you were here
The mirror gives me nothing but pity and fear
My better half, where have you gone?
I sit here in confusion, scared and aware.
I am alone without you.

Alone is Fine

I'm alone and I am fine
Until someone invites themselves into my life;
I give myself away too freely
I get caught up
I get used.
Alone I stand.
Cautious against the wind
Hair whipping into my face
Exasperating breeze blows my clothes against my breast.
Turning tortured triumph
Into lost trust and gained tribulation,
Loyalty misplaced in unfaithful friends.
Beat in the face by my hair
Back to the wind
Screaming inside dying in vain
Living the same
Nowhere to go.
Be proud to be alone.
You were once.
What happened?
Walk away
And don't stop walking;
Long to be touched
Long for the comfort of embrace
Don't give in—
You have too much to lose.
Be alone.
Sometimes
It's the best thing for you.

Aloof Victoria

Alone in her room the mistress sits in despair
Bottle of Jack in her hand reflecting the evening lights' glare
Afraid she has been stood up, wallowing in self-pity,
Opening the door she inhales the scent of the city.
On the balcony in her lingerie —a satin gown of rouge
She stands alone facing the sunset as the purple sky turns midnight blue.
The feel of warm breath on her neck takes her by surprise;
Turned around by her lover —the grip like a vise—
Their lips meet in greeting, their tongues passionately collide,
Their bodies brush together, their fingers intertwine.
To the bedroom she is led, by the hand of her lover
Pulling off her lingerie, turning down the velvet covers.
Putting her arm around her, Victoria sucks her lover's breast
Feeling the warmth in her touch creating wetness
Placing her fingers inside her lover, Victoria begins to moan,
Letting herself be satisfied, letting her feelings show.
From behind, a warm hand caresses her hips;
Victoria glances over her shoulder to see her husband's lips
Not letting her lover go, Victoria lifts her ass into the air
Her husband joins them doggy-style dipping within her soft, wet lair.
Victoria gyrating her hips then puts her face between her lover's legs
Eating her lover's sweet cum while her husband dips deeply slowly within
Then waiting to be treated, lying on his back, he welcomes their attention.
Moaning from the warmth of their tongues on his balls, sweet tension.
Victoria moves her lips up his stomach while her lover caresses his cock
Gently they create a fire within as they get her husband off.
He leaves the two women lying in bed left unsatisfied,
In need. Time for their bodies to be gratified.
Finish my fantasy please?

A Noose

Yeah lady—You are a trip.
Naïve you are not;
You play the game a little too well.
Why do you do that to yourself?
Smile —Nod —And listen for your name
Shut your mouth and open your legs
Walk away once you are done
At least they were not completely denied.
It's when you stay that they start to cry …
Keep that in mind, the next time a buddy comes to fuck
They can't hang the way you can
Their noose is too tight
And yours is too loose!!

And Love It Is

Passionate caress,
I hold tightly to you
Lovingly longing
To need you
To need you

I want to see you with your children
I want to hold you close to me
I want to be your one and only
I want to be your "never leave"

I cannot have these things I want
So I'll want forever to love you
It's all I can do,
Loving me loving you.

Am I to Question

Am I better off dying to live or living to die?
It doesn't matter—why?
Philosophically speaking
We all live to die and we all die to live.
We live for love and fear only.
We love truly and fear honestly.
We will all die—our biggest fear—
Trying to do none other than love.
The four questions placed in my ear
By an eager old man on his way out—
Pen in my hand.
He asks me to answer four questions—
But I don't think I can.
Who am I? Why am I here? Is there a higher being? Does it even matter?

Allow

I need a man who can tell me what's wrong with me
Show me what's right with me
Who will love me for me
To break the cycle of love/hate relationships
Who can give me good love
Let me give good love
Who accepts my willingness to hurt people
The way that I can the way that I do
Don't you say you love me
I do not love you

Another Bad Dream? Not Really

I got into a car accident last night.
It was only a dream.
This lady I know—Jackie—was driving my car
I was in the passenger seat.
She was smashing into everything'
The left side of my car was dented, the right all scraped up.
Then she pushed me out of the car
Into a dark alley where I woke up.
Then I really did wake up—JJ was holding onto me.
I pushed him away. He did not wake up, thankfully.
I fell asleep again, and continued the dream.
In this dark alley I was walking, not getting anywhere.
Then something hit me in the head;
I felt numb then unaware.
My hands were suppressed by a rather large man;
He was holding my legs down with his other rough hand,
I was on my side—he was trying to rape me.
I struggled for a moment, but decided it did not matter;
I could learn from this experience,
It would only make me stronger.
But then I heard a voice, as he undid my pants;
It said, "This won't help you, Amanda,
It's not worth the chance."
I felt a pierce of anger sting just inside my throat—
A burst of adrenaline took over me—
I head-butted him in the nose,
Then I hit him in the throat.
He let go of me, and I struggled to get up.
Then I thought about it for a second,
And I turned around to see
Who was this man who tried to hurt me?
Funny—he looked like me.
Damn, I am glad I woke up.
I realized something though …
I was letting Jackie sit in the driver's seat of my life,
At least some of the time.
The only one who's truly allowing me to hurt?
Is me.
Time to let go—*you* are worth so much more!

Another Sip

Another day—
Another taste—
Oh the smell of you
To taste the sweet divinity—
The tickle on my nose when you are pressed upon my lips
The burning down my throat for the taste I cannot resist
My lips are sticky from the syrup you leave behind
Between sips I wait in angst for the taste I cannot quit
I am addicted, and loving every sip.

Argh, Blech, Ugh!

This straight girl friend of mine showed up early and stayed all day.
She called as soon as she walked out my front door and left a message that
Said, "It's been thirty seconds exactly since I left your side,
And I was wondering if you missed me yet." I called her back and said,
"No, but there are less subtle ways to tell me you miss me, already." Then she
Played the song that rings her phone when I call: Kenny Chesney's,
"You Had Me From Hello." Keep in mind—this girl is *straight.*
Eyebrows raised; "Sure she is." Then I went to class and Filter called
Wanting me to go see her. So I did and this girl was
All over me telling me she wants to try to start a relationship
'Cause I do things to her that even she hasn't felt in
years… She's thirty-something, I'm twenty-something—
Like I haven't heard these lines before? How dumb does she think I am?
Of course she throws in, "I also want to make love to you,
But I can wait until I get to know you better." I throw in the,
"You mean *fuck* me."
She got offended and said, "You know, Amanda,
I don't think I could fuck you; you are too intense and
You intimidate me too much for a fuck.
It would be the real deal if you let me get that close to
You." She tried to kiss me, and she called her best friend, and
Asked her permission to pursue me. Irritated, annoyed, pissed even,
I *had* to leave … Ian called as soon as I walked out of Filter's door, so I
Answered and he invited me to dinner. We went to IHOP,
Talked for an hour or so. I was tired, so I told him
I needed to leave. He asked me to stay the night with him,
Even said he'd sleep on the floor. I said no.
He grabbed hold of me all tight and shit and
Proceeded to tell me he's missed me since he last saw me
And that he had, "waited for the opportunity to hold me."
Argh, blech, ugh!

Artwork: Process versus Product

Creating and straining your brain for each miniscule thought
Of ridicule you could convince yourself to be to true to.
Believe in the false worth of an exaggerated negative ego.

"Get over yourself," say the article's authors:
Believe in that which you are, not which others perceive you to be.
Let down your guard, your inhibition, draw creatively.

As one—the artwork—simply stands alone.
In the front of the room, collectively, creates a personality of its own.

Ten artists perceive in their own way—
All become one in the front of the room.

Naked personalities come into fruition;
Taste the creativity within you.

Bad Day Penny

Representation of the need to think
Actualizing the symbolic lack thereof throughout tomorrow—
Realize that a penny for your thoughts
Equals a day well spent.

Bad Girl, Guilty Mind

I drank a Dr. Pepper yesterday.
I knew better. I should have never done it.
By the end of the day I had had seven of them.
Today I had two.
I have to stop, *right now*.
I know what will happen.
I know what I will do.
I need to stop right now before I can't—
Well, there went that. I'm screwed.

Be Cum One

Lie on your back,
Let me take control—
Put you in my mouth,
Let me be your whore.
Slowly, slowly, deep and wet,
Faster, faster, don't be delicate.
Rub your hand along my thigh
Not too fast. I want you inside.
Turn yourself over and get on top,
Open my legs, shove in your cock.
Breathe deeply into my ear,
Scream out my name so I can hear.
Thrust yourself inside of me,
Feel me, feel me, scream for me.
Grab my hips. Go deep inside,
Cum within; enjoy the ride.

Beautiful

They can't remember what it is they loved
But they'll never forget why it was they left
All the pain and heartache
The sadness which envelopes the senses, steals the light from the day
Makes the sounds of distant beauty simply fade away
She'll never remember the beauty that sadness stole
That which made them draw closer together, that which made them whole.
We are constantly looking for the sunlight through the rain—
Pushing away the cold wetness which saturates our disdain
For once I wish I could allow them to see
That which they all see as pain
I see as true beauty.

Beautiful Princess

Hello my beautiful princess.
How are you this wonderful day?
I am jealous.
Jealous of the sky that envelopes your beauty,
And of the rain that gets to touch your delicate face.
Jealous of the pillow you lay your head upon,
And of the tears that grace your eyes with sadness.
Jealous of all things in life that get to feel your warmth
And erase your pains.
Mostly I am jealous of ignorance.
I know there will never be another to love you,
As I always will.
You will only know what we have
Once it fades away and slips through
Your hands.

Beauty Within Complicated Simplicity

Beautiful flower,
Bloom on
In the solitude of your soil;
Plant your roots to be spread.
Let the sun's light feed you,
Let the stars warm your eve;
Sultry dance in the daylight,
Sleep somberly in the dark of night.
Wilted petal, why have you fallen?
Share with me your pain.
Oh, I see; you fear my presence.
I see, tell me. Tell me?
I fear you will enjoy my beauty so
That you will pick me from my comfort, my home;
You will take me as yours and I will
Lose my true identity.
And so I wilt, to hide my beauty,
So you will choose not to pick me—
Taking my independence—and allow
Me to flourish, alone, for years to come
In the safety of my environment.
I see. Truly, you don't believe
That my admiring you
Could ever change the beauty
Which you possess?
I promise you in this moment,
I will not pick you.
I will keep you safe from harm.
I will cherish you—in safety.
My beautiful flower,
I fear for you now that we have
This understanding.
Because I cannot stop …
The next wide-eyed girl,
Your beauty may fascinate her.
She may pick you,
You may die at her mercy.
I cry for you,
Beautiful flower.
I feel your fear—
Through my soul, I feel you.
If another comes along,
And feels my beauty, as you fear,
And tries to pick me,
Because you leave me here—
It is my fault; I asked you to leave me.
I respect you for listening.
Pray to the sun and the rain,
That the next person will listen too.
Sultry red bud,
Dance in the wind;
I will protect you
For as long as I can.

Been a Long Time

It's been a long time since I quenched my thirst;
It is two in the morning and I need a drink.
Working at 7-Eleven now, it is everywhere I look,
Calling my name, singing to me, I bet it knows I am fighting it
It is beckoning me, "Drink me. Taste the carbonation, the sweet caramel."
Damn it, Dr. Pepper you know me too well.
Thirty-two ounces gone, thirty-two more,
Damn, there's another, and it's almost four.
I get off work at seven and I fear by that time,
I'll have to re-box the Dr. Pepper because it will all be gone,
Damn Dr. Pepper, I was doing so well.
Nine days clean was a really long spell.
Time to get back on this wagon I was on—
What wagon? Seems, my Dr. Pepper is gone!
Time to get a refill … time to go home.

Bent Flame

I am the candle that flickers
In your room when you try to sleep,
I am the spirit that follows you
When your eyes try not to weep.
I create the enticing flame
That burns within your soul.
I believe I am the maiden
Who is now yesterday's whore.
I reveal to you a mystery,
A part of me you may never know.
I am the inner child
Whom you are depriving of her toys.
I, like you, have been abused.
Ripped in two by my own demise.
But unlike you I fight the demons,
And I become the lie.
For your sake, and for the future,
Reconsider what you do.
I know from experience,
You cannot handle all of you.
You are more than you can match;
Back down before you realize
That the greatest power of them all,
Is hidden in your lies.

Between You and Me

Between you and me there is a very thin line
You toe the line on your side
And me, I am balancing on both sides
Me pulling you, you pushing me
Me pushing you, you pulling me
Damn woman, I have a great idea
Why don't we wrap our arms around each other
And two-step this line?
Both of us can lead, both of us can follow
Our line will technically never be crossed
Because we will be walking it together
Until, that is, we walk away
And that will have to be ok
I don't want your forever
I just want your today
Just today
Want me the way I want you to
Tomorrow is another day
I am sure by then I will have walked away

Billion Dollar Girl

Worth a billion
Worked hard for it all
Came up in this world
All alone
Worth a billion
Fighting hard not to fall
Listening to the world's cruelty
Risking it all
Billion dollar girl
Walking away
Crying inside
Dreary day
Billion dollar girl
Has nothing left to say
Running away
The billion dollar girl
Is worth only about a penny

Biting

Biting stinging my indifference …
My dog is barking, I let her in, she wants back out.
Can't win.
In the mood for something else
Haven't figured out what
I love my jobs but can't wait to start teaching full-time.
Not liking that I am so busy constantly running around.
Tired of making myself available …
To you, and you, and you.
I need to become a recluse.
Hide in a hole, never come out.
I dedicate my life to you and you never seem to notice.
You bitch about how everything in your life sucks
You are so damn selfish.
Take a hint my dear …
Everything in this life is not about you.
Or you, or you.
I can't do it any longer.
I will not answer the calls when my phone rings,
I don't care to talk to you,
Don't care for you to talk to me.
Stop calling me with all your drama;
I am busy.

Blindfolded

Through life, we walk blindfolded
One moment we are in control; driving, the road is clear
The next moment torrential downpour, you see nothing
Scarred for life from the terror you fear – Blindfolded behind the wheel.

Guiding others through life—satisfactorily leading, teaching
Then life changes, and blindfolds, guided, being controlled.
Teacher teaching, then being taught, blindfolded, then blindfolded not.
The two become one and an incessant laughter evokes you

Blindfold grows transparent—still there, but less opaque
Freedom grasps your being and control is regained
With the knowledge that you have the choice:
Blindfold, or be blindfolded.

Blue Red Creation

Blue eyes
Blue skies
Blue water
Blue feelings
Blue atmosphere
Blue regret
Blue …
Red stains
Red blood
Red feelings
Red love
Red roses
Red passion
Red pain
Purple stained eyes
Purple blood skies
Purple water feelings
Purple love healings
Atmospheric roses purple
Regret passion purple
… Pain purple

Breathe

Iris … Named the dog yesterday …
Got rid of her today …
Fran called today …
I'm better … Or do you care?
Probably not …
Fuck it, me neither …
Chilling with Cole once again …
He is falling for me
He'd never admit it
Or will he? He'd only regret it.
Going to nights at 7-Eleven
If I make it that far
With all this damn training …
Anxieties are a bitch …
I need a Dr. Pepper …
Or maybe I should just …
Breathe

Busy Again
I am busy again, working three jobs.
Trying so hard to keep my head on right.
Still a full-time graduate student too.

I love being a substitute, and so far I am good at it.
The kids really seem to take to me well.
Busy but enjoyable!!

I love working with my foster son.
So far so good—it will be one year in less
Than two months, and I love him so much.

I like working...
I work with people with severe disabilities,
I'm not just good at it; I enjoy it!

I love Gunner, my best friend of fifteen years.
We aren't allowed to talk; his wife does not like me.
Can't say that I blame her, but I miss him.

I love hanging out with JJ.
Getting to know him is a lot of fun.
He communicates very well, and he is cute too!

My life is going well for now.
No more Dr. Pepper in my diet,
And I have been good to myself.

I have been sleeping at least four hours each night!
That is very good for me!
I am doing all right ...

Busy again
But taking good care of me—
And loving every minute of it!

Candlelight
By candlelight I sleep tonight
Alone
With no one to share
Sadness my true friend
Has always been there

Buying Clothes

Again!
When I was heavy
I had no problem buying clothes.
All I had to do was dress like a man.
I never had a boyfriend,
But life was a lot easier.
Now I am skinny.
I can't find a single pair of pants to fit me.
I don't see this as a problem;
I just don't buy new clothes.
But my boyfriend is determined
To buy me clothes that fit.
I swear, I try to be nice, but I can't anymore.
He bought me a bathing suit.
It was cute. But I am 6 feet tall.
A small is too small, a large is too large, and a medium,
Well a medium goes in my ass-crack like a thong.
So I had to ask him to take it back.
Then he tried again.
He bought me two wrap skirts.
I have worn men's clothing most of my life, because
I am weirdly tall and curvy for a woman.
I have never worn skirts, and I don't really care to.
Regardless, I try on the skirts.
Again he is disappointed.
One skirt doesn't fit around me at all,
The other? Completely see-through,
Not to mention short.
I feel like I am being ungrateful, but
I told him not to buy me any more clothes.
He can't get his money back on the two skirts,
And his feelings are hurt.
My birthday is coming up,
And now he has spent all this money on things I won't wear.
I think at times it would be easier for me to be bigger.
At least then I wouldn't have to worry about clothes.
Hell, all I could fit into then was a men's medium.
And those fit comfortably.
And I did not have to worry about guys' unrealistic ideas
Of my tall frame fitting into a skirt!
What can you do?
Except hurt their feelings, and
Tell them not to buy you clothes again.
I guess it is harsh, but I don't know what else to do.
I am not going to let him waste his money, *again*.

Can't?

Can't make it all go away
I want to watch you drown
Want to watch you fall
I won't though
Every time I see you fall
I hope and I wait
I love and I placate
Woman
If you only knew
You kiss me
And I feel indifferent
Your touch is arbitrary
Monotonous life that I lead
Will get me where I deserve to be
Not me with you not you with me
You may find the one who loves you
But I can assure you it isn't me
Love will find you
You'll see

Can You See?

I can't win.
I am tired of pissing people off.
I hate that I know what I know.
I hate that I have been there and done that.
I hate that what I know means absolutely nothing.
I hate that people are pissed off at me.
I don't know what I am going to do.
Being alone is my friend:
It never gets me, or my mouth, in any trouble.

Chaos

Fighting to be ok; not going to happen.
Will I be happy? Do I have unrealistic expectations?
My stomach is churning—I am longing to sit—naked
With you—and simply watch a movie
I will be happy eventually
Patience is a virtue.
I need to know one thing:
Am I wasting your time?
When all we have is time …
Because you're not wasting mine.
If tomorrow I have to jump the train, it was worth the ride—
And then some.

Catch Up

Seeing a man and then I learn
He is not alone, husband, father
What will I do now?
I need to get the fuck away
From the things I need not feel
Running away again—just like me.
In need of something to keep me here
And it will not be a married man, of that I am sure.
I am not dating him, just fucking him;
We go to dinner and movies,
And we spend time together,
And yeah, we even have feelings for one another …
He told me he loved me; I could not say it back.
I told him I was sorry he felt the way he did.
He said it was fine, that I was just a kid …
He's ten years older than I am.
Mentally, I'm *much* older than he is.
It's a sad truth. I have been hanging out with him since
October, fucking him since January,
Leaving him now … now that I know he is married.
Yuck! I have been played, and I don't like games.
I am walking away.

Challenge Me

I challenge me to a relationship,
One that proves that I am worthy,
One in which I can prove he is worthy—yes, you read that right, I said *he*.
I am ready for the challenge: today, tomorrow,
Two years from now. Let's do it!
No more fucking around with the idea that
I *am not good enough*.
I am you will see. I'll prove it to everyone,
Most importantly? Me.

Challenge Me Less

Why does it have to be that way
go ahead let me go
I don't want it anymore
I need a life that I can handle

Church

I went to church today. I cried.
It is such a hard pill to swallow.
I kicked Matt out yesterday.
I talked to James, who wants to be more than friends.
If he is serious, I might think about it, but
I do not trust him, so I doubt I'll try.
I feel good for the moment, so I will survive.
I am too open-minded. I am learning that it's ok to be so,
Not ok to share it with the world.
I will learn to be quiet. I have to.
Church makes me think.
It challenges me to be something … different.
The one thing I struggle with daily.
Being different …
It has to happen. We'll see where it gets me, if anywhere.
Church makes me think about being a different me.
A me I do not like.

Cole and **the** Burned Bridges

It is interesting the things we do, you doing me, me doing you …
It is interesting because we are night and day,
Yet we are night and night with day and day …
I am the moon still setting when you, the sun,
Have already begun to shine.
Great vision, isn't it?
We still see each other clearly, half the time, maybe more.
We are not that opposite, I am starting to realize,
And so I walk away …
Thinking about you as more than a friend,
The possibility is funny and yet not.
I hate that we cuddle after we fuck …
And yet I don't.
I hate that you call me and we hang out for hours …
And yet I don't.
I like knowing about the other girls,
You've finally started being honest with me …
There is no "and yet I don't" to follow that line …
And only you know why! As I sit here hysterically
Laughing as I see the look on your face
Knowing you know that statement,
Couldn't be more true!
I never think it'll happen, you finally seeing that I am worth
More than a "fuck buddy" thing.
I am so glad that I am hard to read, and that you'll never ask,
Because if you did I might forget …
How it is I feel when I think about—
The things we do, the things we do,
When I am spending my precious time with you …
I feel comfortable with you. Thank you for being
A true friend.
What? Did you think I was going somewhere else with this?
Assumptions get you nowhere. And I am going places!
I am hard to read … remember? Buh-bye.

Condoms Are Easier to Change Than Diapers

Intelligence is hard work, but ignorance will get you into more trouble.
"Slap on your thinking cap before you study."

Dismissing the consequences may feel good,
But you will eventually have to accept them, and that may not.

In the back seat, sixteen and a terror,
But taking the Pill seemed to scare her.
Said she, "Goodness sakes, I don't make mistakes."
In nine months she gave birth to an error.

So the condom doesn't feel good.
Neither does herpes
Neither does AIDS
Neither does being a parent when you're not ready.

Confession of the Sketched Heart

Confused
Torn Ripped Used Played
Being drawn
Erased
Being raped
From the paper
You artist. You painter. You perpetrator. You thief.
Stole the paper
Wasted ink
Drew my heart
Erased its beat
Dying, crying
Trees you've torn
Life is gone
Mastermind
Scorned …

Confused

Confused, in a daze, hate the world, hate this place.
I care not to be in a world as confusing as this.
Interrupted thinking, shattered through, fell for injustice
When I fell in love with you.
Broken mirror, stolen glass, leave me be, for this too shall pass.
If you don't want anyone to know, don't do it.
Spiritually, I am lost; emotionally, I am disturbed;
Physically, I am the composite me—
Basically, I am at the edge and I'm sure six feet is not so far down.
Damn, I've fallen. Does anyone care to lend me a hand?
This hole seems too difficult for me to climb out of on my own …
Oh shit, what is this I see? Happiness here to lend a hand to me?
Thank you for pulling me out of my darkness.
Yes, happiness, I mean you.
I am alive once again.
This time, to myself I will be true.

Consumed

The erratic thoughts consume my head.
Make me wish that I was …
No, never crossed my mind.
Even now I am disgusted by the thought.
Lost myself for a moment …
I'm back. Sometimes I want nothing
But to keep it real. Walk away from the bullshit.
I am so damn good at being alone.
I keep trying to test myself, to be with people—
But I just fuck things up when I do.
I'm spending money—late for work, walking away
From what I care about. I don't understand.
When I'm alone, I do great at work,
Have all my shit together, no complaints.
When I have friends I take them on—completely.
I am late for work, take days off.
Walk away. Stay on the phone. Get taken for granted.
I'm twenty-five; I want to change things, right now,
For me.

Contemplating

I can't live like this,
Nothing to show for the things I do.

I need to rest. I need to sleep
There's a lot I need to do.

What is there in the in the back
Of my mind for you?

In love with the feeling,
But is it true?

I walk away satisfied,
Nothing left to do.

Lost in a moment, dreams in hand
I am in love, and you are the man.

I can't continue this feeling
Sleepless—restless—tortured

I want nothing else
Than to walk away
With
From
You.

Craziness

My life is crazy
It is 11:54 in the evening;
I have been working since 6:00 a.m.
An overnight position right now.
I will get off at 9:00 in the morning.
So, 6 a.m. on the 8th to 9 a.m. the 9th is … 27 hours straight.
Still, life is good. I am tired, but I have bills to pay.
I will make it through this so-called life of mine.
I am in love with a good old friend; I have been for many years …
And it shows. He is married and I have played the good little
Best friend all that time. He asked me to be
Selfish, to be honest, to tell him what I want …
I did, and I felt like shit afterward—and yet
I was proud to get the chance to tell him out loud that I
Would marry him, have his children, be his best friend,
Be his lover, be his temptress, be his everything and nothing
Still. I was relieved to give my heart away.
But I am afraid. I know he is scared.
I know he wonders if leaving is the right thing to do,
I know he fears we won't work out,
I know he fears failure.
But he doesn't know what I do.
He and I have been through everything together:
Divorce, death, love, hate, friends leaving and coming,
finding ourselves, children, family matters … All of it,
And we have done it together. We are not going to fail.
We, he and I, try too hard to succeed. There is no way
He or I would allow the relationship to fail if we took it
To that level … He knows it, and I know it …
He is just scared.
He will always be my best friend …
What do I want? Same as always: nothing.
But if I were asking for anything?
To be a teacher, and a good one, for life.
To be a hard worker at all that I try to do.
To be good to me.
I need that most of all.

Criss-Crossed **You**

Criss-crossed you
I'll take you by the hand
Off to somewhere new
Criss-crossed you

Criss-Crossed you
Take me on this ride
The good and the bad
Criss-crossed you

Criss-crossed you
And I want you to know
Nowhere else I'd rather be
Criss-crossed you

Criss-crossed you
Holding on tight
Not ever letting go
Criss-crossed you

Criss-crossed you
What don't you get?
I'm not leaving—not yet
Criss-crossed you

Criss-crossed you
I'll follow you anywhere
To hell and beyond
Criss-crossed you

Crystal Formation

Crystal water
Brings roaring rapids
Stars in the sky shine brightly
Mountain peaks
Bring powered presence
These are the things
I love

Cuddle

Why can't my beauty come from within?
Or does it?
I am tired and want to cuddle up with you.
And there's nothing I can do
Except sit here and write
About wanting to lie down in bed with you
Maybe someday … but damn
If I don't hate that it felt so right.
I can't explain it, can you?
What happens when game meets game?
You push when I pull
And you have someone else on the side
So when I push you think that's just fine.
I am loyal if only to a fault
So I push and you leave
You push and I pull
This doesn't seem fair to me at all
So now what?
I want to cuddle
Am I worthy of more than just being played by you?
Or do I become just another relationship
In your memory journal to read about
When you brag about where you've been and what you've done?

Cussing

Something was triggered in me today that made me very
Angry. I hung out alone, but not really. I promised myself
I would not cuss, and all day I have been on the
"Cuss a-lot-train." My friend Kelly, whom I have known for over a
Year, hung out with me, and my foster son stayed with me
Today. It was amazing. I haven't had such a good
Thanksgiving in a long time. So why the hell am I so angry?
I am stressed out—shit, my back is sore because of the stress! Fuck, I
Need to go to the ER first thing in the morning because my damn
Stomach has been hurting for three fucking months now, and
I am sick and damn tired and unfortunately not able to cope with it any
Fucking more. I feel so damn stupid for admitting that I am in pain,
But I know what the fuck it is, and I will be better as soon as I see a
Doctor. Fuck, I need a Dr. Pepper—for some damn reason that just calms my fucking
Nerves about the shitty pain I feel … I just got off the fucking
Phone with Lele and she is taking me to the fucking doctor right
Fucking now because she could sense in my voice that
Something was wrong and she freaked …
So I'll finish this fucking thought later.

Daddy Come Home
Daddy, I miss you.
When are you coming home?
Daddy, I need you.
I feel so alone.
Daddy, you should see Mommy;
She cries all the time.
Daddy, I don't understand—
It is such a crime.
Daddy, why did they take you away from us?
We need you here at home.
Daddy, leave that war;
They can fight it on their own.
Daddy, why don't you listen?
Why do you stay away from home?
Daddy, why don't you answer my letters anymore?
I send them once a week.
Daddy, I do not understand;
It is to you I long to speak
Dad. I am one year older now.
This will be the final letter that I write.
Dad, I know the war is over,
And I know you are watching over me tonight.
Dad, I just needed to let you know,
To me you will always be,
Dad—you are a hero,
You mean the world to me.
I love you, Daddy.

Damn It, Me
You are scared, alone and struggling
Dealing with the hurt and guilt from so many;
What are you going to do? Please figure it out quickly.
I am tired of being sad; stand tall, fall short,
Never love, lead me astray.
I know the feelings you feel
And from that I walk away.
Why can't you understand
The way you make me feel?
So many emotions it's just too real.
I do not understand what you want from me
To this life I cry, to this feeling I heal, to you I commit
My demonic portrayal; my heavenly tears fall short.

Damn It, M. C.

I will never understand what it is you want from me.
One minute you call me crying, telling me you love me,
You miss me, you learned so much from me, you need me;
The next, you are blaming me for ruining your life.
Well, don't call me; I don't call you.
Forget about me, and I will forget about you.
You are not with me, and I don't want to be with you.
I have been single since July,
And I am satisfied.
You are the one who longs to be held by another—
But I am not the other who will ever hold you again.
Leave me be.
I will forever love the memories of our time together:
Yes, both the good and the bad.
I do remember the day we tossed the football in the fresh
Snow; it was magical, and mmmmm, Kathy Johns.
I do remember the nights we watched movies, and Pine Acres.
I do remember the fish we helped grow, the apartment in Connecticut,
Our time in Massachusetts. But I also remember the time you told me I was
Not pretty enough to be your girl,
The time you cheated on me with Laura,
The times you stole money from me, the times you lied to me;
Most importantly, the times you told me you would
Try not to hurt me again.
All of them.
I love you forever, but only as a friend.

Damn It, Tony

I am sorry you feel like I should just lie down and
Spread my legs for you, but I am not your whore.
I know you are scared, you are alone, and you think I will
Be great for a fuck, but really—who do you think you are?

You are just my roommate, just my friend—never more.
Not now, not ever.
Stop telling me I will change my mind. Stop telling me to let my guard down,
And for *fuck's* sake stop crawling into my bed while I sleep!
You are really crossing every boundary.

I put a lock on my door today.
The only problem is I can't keep you out of the house—you still live here.
I have told you no a million times, and you keep saying, "That will change."
The more you say that, the more I don't want you around.
Damn it, Tony, *leave me alone*.

Damn It, Man

I do love you, man, but what do you want from me?
You are a married man. We tried for a while to be together,
But it never would have worked.

Please stop telling me you love me; please stop telling me you miss me;
And for goodness' sake, please stop telling me you want to
Make love to me.

You are married. Go make love to your wife.
Embrace her, and leave me be. Please.
Your family despises me. I will never be your girl.

Stop dragging me along, stop calling, stop e-mailing.
Go love your wife; be grateful for what you have,
And realize this most importantly:

You are not in love with me,
You are in love with the best friend
I have always been to you.

I will forever be your best friend, but that is all
I can be. I am not good enough for you,
You really don't even know.

All I have ever been good at is being capable.
I am a survivor. I take care of people.
You are one I love to take care of,

But I cannot be tied down to you …
I love you entirely too much to ever be yours.
It hurts less that way.

Damn, You've Got Me

Twisted on the image of you and me
Together, intense—the foundation poured

Intermingled building wrapped in a fence.
Me—just a figure a brick to help you stand tall.

Standing back, watching, letting me observe;
Just another brick in your wall.

Damn It All

Ain't it kind of funny that
At the dark end of the road
There is always a light to guide us?
Say it isn't so.

I will eventually understand why I am so passionate about life,
Why I let so many people grace me with their presence,
Just to let them all go.

I will eventually understand what it is I am here for …
I know I will live forever, because my word is printed,
Never to be erased by another. I have been immortalized

I know I will live forever because I will
Donate my organs to someone who needs them,
Surviving through them and their families.

I know I will live forever, because I strive to
Be a great teacher of life, and I know for a fact I have
Taught many unsuspecting students.

I will live forever, damn it,
Because I strive to do so, and I refuse to fail.

Damn That

Stop telling me what you want, stop saying you love me—
You truly don't see, it do you? You are not alone—
You are not the only bitch on my telephone—
What do you mean, you want to see it?
Girl, now I know you must be trippin'!
See my list—shit, let me see yours!
I am not your fucking whore—
So what if my phone rang nine times
While we were together?
How do you know it wasn't the same person every time?
You need to stop assuming before you lose your mind.
Yeah, I want a lover, that's true,
But I'm telling you up front it won't be you.
It will be a man and I will settle down
Once I find some common ground.
Until then I play and not for keeps—
So shut up, drop your pants and let me fucking eat!
I'm tired of waiting already … Women.

Dawn

If with men, in love, you don't succeed,
Fuck what the world thinks, and fall in love with me.

Dear God

I am in need. We all are.
People always ask why I do not pray to you,
Why I do not worship you as they do.
I hate being selfish. I do not want to bother you.
There is so much pain and suffering—you do not need my fears, my anxieties …
But if I were to disclose to you what I am thinking …
I would say to you this:

> I do not want to be scared anymore. I fear attachment, even to you.
> I do love unconditionally, and I hope to someday be someone's true love.
> I want so intensely to be given the chance to be a foster mom.
> I want so badly to be good at all I do.

To succeed
To be a good teacher
To be involved in the life of a child
To grow up
To be strong emotionally
To be able to calm my own anxieties
Most importantly—To be happy.

> I am sorry that I won't confide in you for fear of being selfish. I am sorry.
> I am happy. But I do need …

Deceit

Calling on the phone, making sexual gestures.
Speaking of the unforgivable, loving each moment.
Becoming erect, not letting go.
Scared of the moment when the secret gets out.
Playing sexual games—such a tease.
Wondering if life would be better if someone knew.
Knowing the secrets must be kept.
Turned on by the thought of sharing herself.
With more than one man, with more than her dreams.
Passion takes over; loneliness grows stronger.
Longing to join her partner. Fighting off the urge.
Alone in her bed. Pleasing herself.
A knock on the door brings a pleasant surprise,
A familiar face with a clever disguise. Invitation opens.
Alone in the silence, unforgettable pleasure.
Fear of someone finding out, fear of not being pleased.
Sitting alone talking. Choosing to lie down.
A simple kiss on the neck—sinful. An even simpler touch going further.
Being pleased-scared of the truth. Longing for more.
Afraid of the pleasure principles. Waking up. Deceived.

Decisions

I have had to make many decisions in my lifetime
I am a smooth-talking criminal
I can steal the thunder
I will steal the clouds
I am a thief of the night sky
I have taken your love and
I have made it mine
I am good to my gifts
I have seen you see my reaction
I will be just as careful with you.
I have made my decision—to love you
I will no longer fear you leaving me
I understand now—until I lose you—whether now, or in fifty years.
I cherish you …
I have made my decision—and my decision is you.

Demanding

Demanding too much, too soon, gave you a corpse for a child,
Because now I feel worthless and incapable for
Not being able to follow through, and
I feel like I let you down.

Denied Intoxication

Walk away from the fuck toward the pain I create in myself

It's not worth the hassle, the chaos of your lies.

Tip back the bottle of fear and resentment.

Hate the burn as it engulfs me.

Lay my head upon your beating heart, envelop you with all of me.

The pain begins to subside as our bodies become one.

The smell of your heat lingers as I curl my fingers around your bottle.

Roll my head back, swallow. I am satisfied once again.

Put down the bottle; stop the blood's effervescent flow.

Fuck once again. Do not burn me with your emotions.

You can't understand me—don't expect me to understand you.

I just want to make love—to fuck it all.

Grab your bottle—deep within me.

Feeling the push—loving the shove.

Teeth around my neck as you break my tears away from me.

Fuck me with your love,—do not try to conquer me.

Touch me, taste me, devour my sweat.

Please me—using you, you make me fucking wet.

My bottle is empty again.

<u>**Different**</u>

You don't need to worry, I know …
You did not change, only I saw it differently.
You weren't different, really, and that is ok.
And I know last night was different, because I was different.
You and I touched differently, moved differently,
You allowed your feelings to be free.
And when you laid yourself on me, wrapped your arms around me,
And held me with a death grip after you were through …
You, me, all of it was so different from the usual …
You will never see, don't care to understand,
And yes I know, only in my mind does it matter.
And yes, I know, if you ever did see, it would ruin you and me.
You act as if I am like them, the drama queens,
You don't like it when I talk; say my opinion never matters,
And all because I asked how your day was, and you told me.
And when I laughed at the fact that you had a bad day,
Said they are all bad, with good elements,
You rolled your eyes and made some snide remark—
You always do—you act as if you are better than me,
And I am no good for you.
And I am in the way once you get what you want,
And only when you are fucked up are you real …
You are so good at the facade.
You insist on hiding as I hide from everyone.
You insist you know me, and yet you don't know me at all.
And I am strong, I will not falter.
You asked me why I got up to leave at 4:51 a.m.,
Said it's too early, you didn't understand …
I did not care to explain; the truth is I was uncomfortable;
I realized it was not different.
You were no different; it was all in my head.
You are only different when you are real,
You are only real when you are fucked up,
And I knew I had to leave—the tension ran too deep.
Even that was no different.
You will never see, never understand.
You always get what you want,
And I will always lend a hand,
Continue to be your servant—you, the master with the plan.
You will continue to call me,
You will continue to see the crass me who could never care
You will always get what you want …
But I will always have the upper hand.
I will smile when we are through,
And I will know what I have done, and you will never do.

Disappearing Ink

My emotions on the concrete in shadowed form
Like ink spilled from its bottle sinking slowly into the cracks on the sidewalk
I reach for it; grab at it, staining my fingertips—vile betrayal,
My hope stands true for your voice to linger on the wind
Call out to me as I stain my hands black with my dejected emotions
I struggle frantically to grasp at my spilled feelings—needing them desperately
I scratch at the concrete, curse the sun for drying out a part of me
Yearn in earnest to retrieve all of me in one fell swoop—my hands—black, denied, Painful
from my wretched failure …
The sun is gone, covered by darkness—clouds—
The sky opens above me and the rain beats my emotions
Splashing them, making them run, spread, hide.
I stand by—hands held out to be cleansed by the rain.
Stains on my clothing from my splashed feelings.
I—failed—realize my loss—walk away.
Cleansed by the rain, I know it is ok.
Start again—with new emotion, white, innocent—free.
All I have to do is change my clothing.

Disturbed Indifference

I should not want to spend my time with you,
But I can't help but think
It's as good for you as it is for me
The outcome is not really important.
My time spent with you—is, why?
Because you and I are all wrong.
I don't like to worry about anything
But I am consumed by you
Excruciatingly painful
What a wicked game we play
Over and over in our heads:
Disturbed indifference—loving her, wanting me.
I know the outcome—come now, come later, it will come out.
Goodbye will come, just as quickly as hello.
But it will be so much more difficult to say
You have a gift for loving me
And I have the perfect present of understanding—you.
Unconditional love—and not for me—I know where you are going.
You consume me. I can't wait to hold you forever
As a memory, as a presence, as a lover, as a friend.
I will hold you forever; you just haven't realized it yet.
You disturb my indifference.
I will walk away disturbed,
And you will walk away … indifferent.

Divine Maturation

In the moment I cried for those who needed my tears
I felt weak, hopeless, my colorful world suddenly bleak
Walking, feeling, such an emotionless keep,
Looking for a way out of the veto
My world spinning torridly out of control.
You! It is because of you that I feel these things
Lying on a bed of your emotions:
Sadness—like walking naked through cold dense fog
Happiness—oh, the smell of a sleeping baby's breath.
Terror—the nightmare of drowning that you just can't wake from
Passion—the first kiss on the fresh glass of the sweetest red wine.
Oh, how you ripped my soul to pieces with all of you.
Scattered, shattered, torn in two. You smothered me
With your blanketed love—me in your bed, covered
I am free now from your chaotic life
No longer will you beat me with your words
Bruise me with your lies
Go ahead and hit me with your emotions—go ahead and try.
I have matured—and it is divine.
I no longer need your love, no longer need your lies.
I am stronger now—and you are left behind.
The feelings I conquer now—sublime.
Like a rose without its thorns, nutrients denied
Wilted feelings lost; I no longer need the fight to survive
My soul is revived, and happiness I will find—without you.

Divinity

I'm doing it again: not taking care of me.
Doing everything to pay my bills—carefully.
I haven't slept in days, I'm not eating right
Worrying about money, diabetes, and my girl all night.
What's all this got to do with the things in my life?
Someday I will be happy
One day things will be right
Right now, I have one need,
One important, opportunistic thing
I need to be hopeful for many things
My foster=care project, the children in need
My life as it stands right now,
The way of everything.
Bringing me down
Can't anyone else see?
I know what I must do, I know what it is I need
I need to find the faith within me.
Divine, divine, divinity.

Division of Geologic Chronology

Time is ubiquitous and yet there is no timeline for it.
You cannot define it. You cannot stop it. You cannot
Re-create it. Time is a handcuff no one has the key for—
Always alone and surrounded by people.

Don't Change

Sitting here at work with nothing I'd rather do
Than waste away my time just thinking about you.
Yeah, you're fucked in the head; I am too;
Hell, it's what intrigues me most about you.
You will understand, someday you will see,
What people love about you, love
about me.
I know I'm fucked up, and I know people see
How much pain I can cause them, but they truly believe
Though I cause pain, I'm not as bad as they first perceive.
You, my dear, are just like me;
You draw them in, knowing what they see.
The only difference is,
I love me for me, and you just can't conceive
Why anyone would love you, or love me.
But let me ask you one question, if I may be so bold:
Why do you stick around? Why haven't you gone away?
Oh wait, I know …
It is because you love that I love me,
And all those things you hate about you,
I have learned to love about me.
Right?
One day you'll learn …
Oh, but on to better things.
I love what you are; don't try to change you …
Would you want to try to change me?

Don't Feed the Birds

Don't feed the birds or they will come back
Unwanted lovers come home to feed
Even when the seed has long been rotten

Don't Judge

Don't judge me tomorrow
For the way I'm acting today.
Want to know more about me
I'm the girl who is sweeping you off your feet
But don't judge me now for the way I'll act in two minutes,
Because I may not be so sweet.
As a matter of fact,
I know I won't be.
I've been sweeping people off their feet for years.
Guess what—you aren't any different.
I'm sorry I made you feel special
Guess what—you're not.
You are just like the rest of them
Fell right along with the best of them.
Told you what you needed to hear
Made you feel good —
Let you go.
And you didn't see it coming.
All alone you stand with the rest of my followers
Hands in your pocket,
Head spinning
Don't you know why you are confused—it's ok.
I do
And I don't regret it
Or what I did to you.

Don't Try

Not in the mood to be figured out by you
The more you try the angrier I get
Lost in the thought that you can't figure me out
And believe me, if you do, I'll change to spite you yet.

Don't act like you see what's going through my head.
I won't believe that you could ever know
Why do you try so damn hard? I'm not yours.
You love her, and I'm not good enough—so go.

Leave me the fuck alone; I'm not in the mood
My life changes constantly and you won't be true
Part of you, part of this thing called me—worrying, leaving.
Leaving now, not for me baby, for you.

Doomed by My Mojo

Doomed to walk alone in this world forever
An over-achiever, my life not defined by all I do
I meet new people daily, but very few people stick around
Once they start to get into my brain, and figure me out
They run away with their tails between their legs.
Four years in the Army
I am a published author
I am finished with my Masters,
I am a teacher and a learner,
I am trained in welding, auto-body repair, mechanics, massage therapy
None of it matters to me
Those are things that go on my resume;
They do not define me,
They certainly do not show people how I love.
Lately I have begun to think I could give it all up, trade it all for a moment—
Every time people tell me they are not on my level, it makes me sick.
What does that mean? I do those things for me …
So I can be proud of me …
Don't we all do this?
Guys seem interested and then I get,
"You are too much for me,
But that doesn't mean we can't be awesome fuck buddies."
I have spent my short little life literally living like today will be the last,
I have everything I have wanted
Except one thing: true friends
They say I have accomplished too much in too little time
I try too hard, I am too creative
What?
Do I have to pretend I am something I am not—
Just to earn people's friendship?
Are people honestly that shallow that I can't accomplish what I want in life,
And still have true friends?
What are we living for if not to sacrifice, love, hate, feel, accomplish,
Make friends, make enemies, and—
Heaven forbid—
Die happy with the things we have accomplished?

Drama

I have endured so much
For no apparent reason.
It's sad.
The things I deal with
Simply because I don't say no.
How I would love to be able to tell people
To go away.
I can tell myself not to feel passion or love
Or anything at all for that matter.
But—of course—I can't tell people to go away.
It just doesn't work out for me.
The passion is gone. I turn it off.
I avoid the emotions others try to convince me to feel.
The passion, the fire, disappear.
How do I tell them that I am not interested?
I don't.
It's really not even worth the drama.

Dress to Undress

Dressed in black velvet with you in my thoughts
I lay upon my bed, create wetness, touch the spot
Fingers inside myself, warmth envelopes my skin
Knock on my door interrupts my fantasy
The door opens gently
It is you I see,
The laughter of eroticism
Fills my living room as I walk to where you stand
You smile ever so, as I reach for your hand
Replacing my hand with yours
With your fingers I caress
My salty wet rose
With such intense eagerness
Without hesitation
You pull my body to yours
With a kiss and a smile
You pull me to the floor
Undressing my body
With your hands
With your teeth
I wrap my body around you
For a sharing of the feast
Both of us naked,
I turn you on your side,
Slip your cock inside of me
With a wicked, sexy moan…
Finish my fantasy

E Pluribus Unum

Everything unconditional is conditioned through life
As we see it
Perfection is the realization that everything is imperfect
As we see it
Disbelief cannot happen if you do not believe
As we see it
Humane does not matter without inhumane
As we see it
I believe life is based on:
Necessarily unnecessary
Perfectly imperfect
Satisfactorily unsatisfactory
Usually unusual
And I believe most importantly in the knowledge that it is
As we see it.
To say that you are not creative shows creativity
No matter what we say, no matter what we feel
Life is as it is and it is all that is real
And that is the basis for all ways of seeing
Out of many, one.

Eye

Emerald
Sapphire
Creates my desire—
Run—run—run to me
Free yourself—into my arms:
Free me, free me.

Easter I Don't Celebrate

In this world where everyone conforms
And only I am different
I feel the eyes upon me
In this room alone
Struggling with divorce, graduation,
Love life, love life,
Despair, regret, imagination, tenets
I am randomly confused
Holding tightly to the sinister secrets
I have none, but one,
I am married to a loser, and dating someone …
Love life, love life,
Until my divorce is final,
From a man I haven't seen in years, I have to sit here all alone
And wallow, and play, in my own crestfallen tears
I deserve better than this superficial life
One man forever, not many for a night
Love life, love life,
Water of crystal blue, carry me away
Take me to the coven in which the maidens play
To sail in the depths of the effervescent sea
Free me of the sedentary, secular world
Free me, free me, let my happiness soar away
Love life, love life,
What I want in this nonconformist mindset
Let me live my life, not yours
Easter will not go away
Just because I do not celebrate
I am not a sinner; I do things my way
Love life, love life,
Hell, at least I have a life; I could be underground
With maggots crawling through my head
I know I am a non-traditionalist
To me, it isn't worth being part of the group
Because then I'd have to judge me, like you do
Love life, love life,
From the time I started having these thoughts, until now.
I realized I should not feel guilty for being different
It is me, regardless
So I guess I will go, give my boyfriend a kiss
To hell with Easter, my husband, and all the conformists
Live life, love life …

Education

Formal education? A marketing scheme
All people are teachers, even if they never willingly teach a thing
Controlled environments, all-day day care …
Children go to school, parents work, economically profitable …
Educate. More jobs, more money, more workers to hire
Formal education, what is it really about, and why?
A rhetorical question; I already know the answer is not important.

Emotionally Bare Naked Aware

The endless possibilities of a love that will never be.
So careful, so careless, so absolutely free.
Constantly searching—will I be searching for life? I hope not.
If I find it—will I be strong enough to see
The good and the bad so that I do not
Fear leaving of my own accord?
Sleeping naked to take advantage of you—
I'm not sure yet what I think.
I know I will crash today.
Get up at three, do my homework. Go to class.
Maybe go home and get more sleep.
I don't care to do much more.
Work—sleep. Pay off my bills.
That's the life I want for me. No one will ever see.
I have such incredible standards … but they fit …me.

End of Semester

There is so much to do in the end of the semester.
Every day is full, every night is restless.
I don't seem to have enough time to do the things I want
But I have plenty of time to do the things that need doing.
Oh well. I am enrolling for classes for the summer and fall.
I keep holding onto the thought that in less than three weeks
I will be finished with school.
I will be free of homework.
I will try to fill my time tutoring because it pays more,
And I think it will be more rewarding.
I am wonderful. It is a stressful time of year,
But I expect that the summer will be much better.
All is well.
I am in love;
My jobs are doing well;
I will work on my stress;
I will succeed.

Eradicated Truth

When the time is right,
The bird will deliver its message,
With love, hate, sadness,
Eradicated truth …
The pendulum swings in both directions.

Everyone

Everyone is so scared of getting hurt.
I am not.
Not getting hurt would mean
I never loved anything enough to care.
I am not sure what would hurt more?

Evidence

I have not done anything quite like this before
I am going to be painfully honest with you
Because I love you.
I have to use comparisons; they are all I have.
First love never felt good enough to make it forever.
It was too complicated to be right.
Second man I never even told him I loved him.
He was just too damn dependent on me.
The third we got married because we were
Scared of being alone—and we knew it.
I can't help but think about forever;
I am not even scared.
I am willing to get hurt if
Need be. The way I feel when I am with you
Is satisfyingly wonderful. Holding you, looking into
Your thoughts, talking … just lying together without
Saying a word … is this love?
Because if it is, I can assure you,
I've never been on this train
Before. If you feel like we need to put the
Brakes on—do it … I will understand.
You and I have such a bond that even if you
Walked away, I truly believe you would love me
Forever. I know, without reservation, that until eternity
Ends, and forever begins, you will hold a special place
In my heart—whether you are with me or not.
Words cannot express it; forever is just not
Long enough to show you.

Evil Prevails

Looking at you through the photograph
I swore I saw myself
But when I took a closer look
I saw the demons from hell
Black and white good and evil—
The picture came to life
Evil written in black
Innocence in white

Looking at you through the photograph
I swore I saw myself
Until I took a closer look
And saw the demons of hell.
Doorway reflecting darkness
Flowers potted in white
dark shadows hovered the earth
Stars shone through the windows
Two-dimensional layers

Looking at you through the photograph
I swore I saw myself
All alone standing
Sad as the doorway's binding
Holding camera in hand
Hearing my demon calling me
Pleading for me to set my demon free

Looking at you through the photograph
I swore I saw myself
Until I took a closer look
And saw my ragged self
Hidden in the photograph
My evil clone will stay
Two-dimensional catastrophe
Behind the paper—portrayed

Exhausted

I am tired. Have been for weeks.
My years of insomnia finally catching up with me?
No. I am sick, but it is my secret …
I know what it is, but I will deal when I am ready.
My secret Exhaustion is becoming truth …
No longer a secret, it is starting to show.
I better fix it quick, before anyone else knows.
Damn, I hate going through this alone.
I've done it before. I'll do it again.
Exhaustion …
Sacrifice myself once more to the doctors and their needles …
I just don't know.

Exist

The future is a place
That does not exist
But I exist in you

False Plans

What they all want for me
I sit and wait for the day to come
When I will find my special one
The one and only to complete me—
Bullshit. I wish the world could see
There is no such thing.
This one single being
Not one thing will complete me.
It takes so much to be my friend
To stick with me through to the end
If at all possible, that is what I want:
A friend in love, a lover not.
I do not intend to settle down if I can help it.
God's plan does not include a ceremony and a certificate
I do not need your heart and or your ring,
A symbol no less, of lesser things.
I am in need of much.
Many to complete me.
No one will understand,
No one will see. I am in love with no one,
And no one will be in love with me.
That is the way I enjoy my life,
That is the way it has to be.

False Rain

Rain on the windows beating away my indifference.
Lost in the suffocation of my heart pounding in rhythm.
To free myself from my heart's grasp.
Wrapped in panic—rapture—euphoria—fear.
Rapping on the window—constant—never ending.
Longing to be running through the field—
Looking, searching for you to see—to see me.
Why not me?
Apparitions from my past—I am missing something.
All these ghostly women, men, children, walking around,
Searching for something to see—searching for me?
To be back in my house, thunderous pain,
Windows beaten to death by the unfeeling rain.
Drowning in the feeling—you—me.
Waking up from this dream within a dream
Feeling your skin pressed against mine—
Pouring rain—your heart's beat.

Feeling Beautiful

In my room feeling beautiful.
Tranquility cast upon my body.
Feeling euphoria—sadness—loneliness.
No one to call. No one to share this with.
I am beautiful, sad.
Want to shed these tears that envelop my heart.
Can't seem to find my reason to be loved
Every one of them lusts for me.
None wants to be more.
What is it about me?
Love that I am sensual.
Love that I am me.
Sad that I am alone,
Sorry that I am lonely.
I could use a hug.
Or a smile.
Or you making love to me.

Field of Red

There I wept on the battlefield
Around so many of my friends
For death had taken on a new face
As he reared his ugly head.
No birds chirped nor did the plentiful flowers grow
For what appeared beneath my feet
A field of red blood flowed
Surrounded by the innocent,
The strong and lonely tears
The muscle of the weapons,
The ammunition's glow
From hilltop to grassy knoll,
The sparkle of death unmistakable
What they died for no one knows.
As the stench of fear from the warriors
Cut through the sullen mists
Alone I wept for the fallen
In a field of red lifelessness
I wondered what set them free
Was it the rain cleansing their souls
Or the call of military duty?
Looking back it doesn't matter
I am alive but they are free
The riddle of war haunted by fields of red
They all lost their fight for life
Yet I am the one who is dead.
The answer to the riddle of war
Where no one really wins
Is if there is a field of red
It is such from ignorance.

Five in the Morning

I am off work today;
Shouldn't I be sleeping?
Should be—I am tired.
If I could sleep right now, I would.
I want somebody to hold.
How sad.

Fire One Day, Ice the Next

I am a proud person. I have way too much to lose,
If I stay forever alone, I will not lose my pride for you.
You assume you know me,
Told me I was an easy one to love,
You've known me for twenty-four hours,
Asked if you could kiss me after knowing me for twelve.
In the first eleven hours I was on fire, playing,
Cutting jokes, open as a house with no frame,
Then …
You lay down in my bed to talk to me,
Wanted me to hold you,
Talk to you, be with you …
Told me you couldn't handle how awesome I am.
Put your arms around me and I pulled away.
I know you are a virgin … You told me, and that I believe.
I don't think it matters that you are twenty-three.
I just know you want a relationship, and that is not for me.
So yeah, we had a really good time.
But you really are better off with someone else,
I could only mess with your mind.
I am doing this for your own good …
Don't look at me with those sad eyes.
No, I will not hug you, touch you, kiss you instead …
You are better off without me,
And I'd rather be alone in bed
Goodnight, and goodbye.
As I walked you to the door, you protested
Confused about my change in mood
Have my ice; my fire is dead.
You are one of the good guys; most girls eat that shit up.
Go buy her a rose, open her door,
Hold her while you are sleeping, and give up the thoughts of you and me.
I am not for you to keep.
I'm not the kind of girl you take home.
You are way too naïve for me.

Fierce Waters

Fierce waters flow
Beneath me
My body soaked in vain
His silky skin envelopes me

Our souls commit such sin
Fingers running wildly
Over pieces of me—
Through him

Kisses of
Forbidden desire
Create exotic dances
Beneath the wind

Fierce waters flow
Through me
Wash me away
Him in my arms

Call out my name
So the heavens may hear
Tell me storm clouds
I may commit this sin

Create a magnificent display of bright
Lightning cast from my creation
Watch me take him passionately
In me, in me, deeply, wetly

Deep thrusts of water
Take us to the shore
Waves rocking our bodies
Moves us to the core

Fierce waters collectively love us
Generate a desire untold
Let us be your vision
Let Satan's dreams unfold

Fierce waters calm beneath us,
Hold us in your warmth
Take us to your coven
May we be your story untold

Flip the Script

Mmm … The smell of you
Lying warm in your arms
To see your tender eyes
Shining, smiling back at me
What is it you long for?
What is it you see?
Lying naked, you in my arms
Warmth surrounds my effervescent being
I am intoxicated by you.
Strange how the little things
Make me so fucking happy
Not even your angry words
Could make me walk away …
Maybe—maybe I *have* felt this way before—
Maybe I will feel this way again—
Why can't you just accept that I feel what I feel right now?
I am sure you have felt similar to this before
Or you would not have gotten married
I am sure that I have felt similar to this before,
Otherwise my relationships would have been based on false pretense
I am positive that the way I feel at this moment is *our* love.
Yours and mine—together—alone
We have such a magnificent strength in each other—that—
What does it *matter* what we've felt before?
Why can't it just matter what we feel right now.
I love you
I am sorry if that is not enough for you.

Fool

Screw you for making me feel this way!
You choking my indifference.
Now what do I do?
Do I just walk away and forget about you?
Haven't we already proven that is not going to happen?
No way to contact you except in these memories of mine …
You and me, lying on the ground, your hand in mine …
Picture perfect, yet,
I have nothing to show …
You are just like the rest, willing to give me so much, and I just let you go.
I do this every damn time! I warned you: you let me fuck with your mind,
And now I am the one who cannot release the anger within me …
I love you, but only, as a friend.
No other way will do …

For You and You and You

Do I think about you all the time?
Well—no. Am I supposed to?
Do you think about me all the time?
Is that what you are actually getting at?
If it is, ok; just be straight with me.
When I think about you, I only think about how we
Hit it off and how we could be great friends. I think
About the way I felt with your hands on me, your tongue in
My mouth and your words in my ear. But I don't think about
An "us" that isn't there. You pretend to be a player just
Like me—but you seem to want so badly for me to fall for
You … I truly don't understand.
Honey, no players playing players' games. I'm hard to get,
But once you have me, I am loyal, and I am kind. Until
Then, I will continue to mess with your mind …
Tell me what it is you think I want—and we can work on it
From there. Drop the psychological bullshit and love me
For me—not for what you want me to be—and we will
Go far. And not for what you think you see. Do not
Assume—just ask if you want to know—and my answers
Will be true. Start being real with me.

Foreplay

Sitting at the table
Working
Watching you walk by.
The look in your eyes says you want me—
And I am ok with that.
The thought of your tongue on my lips,
Your flesh upon my soul—
I'm trying to cry out.
Yearning for more.
I don't care what they say.
This is for me—for you …
Someday.
Until then,
Our eyes commence
In
Foreplay

Forget

Forget the pain as it flows through you;
Walk away from the emotions that fill you.
Anger consumes your sad heart …
You struggle with that.
Forget that you might matter—
Know that you don't.

Foundations

All my life, I have been building foundations.
Pouring my concrete all over the world.
I never seem to make it past the foundations.
Cleverly, something always happens to change my plans.
My world is filled with incomplete foundations.
Here I am, moving again. Foundations laid, plans failed.
Alas, I have decided, I will lay no more foundations.
I am on my way to the nether world, foundations or no …

F and S

F: "I …"
S: "I am—"
F: "I am calling …"
S: "To?"
F: "To tell you about a girl."
S: "About a girl?"
F: "About a girl named Poetry."
S: "What are you talking about?"
F: "I …"
S: "Don't you start that again."
F: "I called to tell you about a girl named Poetry, with whom I'm falling in love ."
S: "A girl named Poetry?"
F: "But there's one thing standing in the way."
S: "Oh, and what's that?"
F: "Well, I am in love with …"
S: "Don't even think it! If that statement ends with '*you*,' I don't want to hear it."
F: "I figured—I gotta go, and I won't be back. You've lost your chance."
S: "Go then. See if I care."
F: "There's that damn wall again. I don't even know why I tried. I love you. Goodbye."

Free Will

In with the new
Out with the old
Millennium is here
I feel for the world
Introduce into the air
A love for all things
Whatever happened to unconditional
I am trying
I love by a different set of rules
I live by my own set of dreams
I am nobody's bonsai
You cannot manipulate me
Try as you may
Say as you will
I am free
Let me go
I will conquer
On my own

Freedom

Do you think we are educating for freedom? Should we?
Some believe freedom is being taught in school.
Others believe you should teach children there is a certain way to be.
Who are we to qualify freedom? What defines
Freedom and the right or wrong way to teach it?
Some believe there is freedom, but you have to explain it;
But does this guarantee freedom—or just a lesson plan?
Politically, education strips you to believe what is and is not.
Holistically, educated societies have been free
Afforded the right to learn
What they want you to know.

Freedom Fighter

Having to hold a sacred virginity, my dreams are my secrets,
My untouched vicinity.
I am a lover, a dreamer, a creator by heart;
My life brings a lot of obstacles to break this strong heart
I fight and I fight. And the battle goes on.
I will win this one day…

Freedom's Rules

The term freedom is no more free than you or I
Just like those people who waste our time
Letting us vote as if it actually counts
Like the killing we perceive to be wrong …
Killing the innocent and the free
As long as a soldier is doing it, it can't be wrong
They're just doing what the government told them to do
Killing motherfuckers under orders
Living the rest of their life with the image before them
Carrying the guilt and the sin forever in their hearts
Freedom, you call it; I say it's bullshit
It's all about the way we perceive it
Freedom is no more free than you or I—
Ironic, isn't it?

Freedom Ain't Free

Fuck all y'all
Who think we're free
Or that the president
Gives a shit about you or me
You live in a land full of false dreams
You'll stick your finger in a fan
Just to see if you bleed
From what I know
From what I see
I live in the same place as you
And baby I bleed
So stick my finger in the fan
Turn the motor on low
Run for cover baby
The motor will blow
Strength within me comes from the truth
That the president don't give a shit
About me or you
You live in a land full of false dreams
The reason I know
Is cause freedom ain't free

Freedom Came Knocking

Lost in the darkness
Of the American dream.
Freedom calls, desires scream.
        Wrapped in the warmth
Of the American flag,
Hugging the freedom, serendipity.
        Longing to be wrapped
Within freedom, within you,
Blessed by the challenge of peace holding true.
        Soaring above heights unseen,
Feeling the wetness,
Pressured dream.
        Wrap your lips around me,
Feel the tightness of my skin,
Hold tight to the freedom,
Calling me, touching you, creating sin.
        Fireworks create,
Naked bodies collide,
Screaming into the night,
Freedom ride.
        Tempting taste,
Sucking on your lips,
Moving with your rhythm,
Gyrating hips.
        Sweat being created,
Screams fill the room,
Soaking in wetness,
Freedom rings true.
        You tell me you love me;
I want to say it too
You ask me for my hand
Waiting for my, "I do."
        I love you girl,
But not right now
I am torn between freedom
And society's shackles
        I want to untie the knot
Society has around me
Wrap you up forever in my arms
But desire is not free.
        So many things in this life
I want for me:
Babies, teaching, respect,
With you, it can't be.
        I'll hate myself forever
For what I am about to say to you:
Society and their handcuffs win.
Baby girl, I just can't be with you.

Amanda Suddeth

Frozen

Walk away from me because I am not perfect.
Or care for me because I am not perfect.
Not wanting to make you love me.
Freedom calling me under her wing—
Screaming to me, catch me?
I walk toward her angelic presence
The coldness of the day creates a terror within.
Snow falls all around—slowly, sadly—I try
I walk away. Freezing to the ground I become
A stationary piece of eye candy for all to gawk at.
One day wish for the sun to shine upon me—
And melt this fair façade. Set me free
Set me free—freedom tried,
Independence encapsulated me.

Fuck Motherfucker

All about the drugs and the booze
I need friends who are a lot different than you.

Bill—Neil—Paul—Victor … All of you …
Coke, alcohol, marijuana … I can't deal.

I am clean, and I don't want ya'll around.
That shit ain't for me.

Ya'll make me uncomfortable.
I want to be free from you all.

No more chillin' @ my house.
Don't come around please.

Bill, you are the one I need to get rid of 4 now.
Fucking making me uncomfortable I tell you I don't like alcohol

I tell you I don't like pot—you smoke—while I am around.
I tell you it makes me uncomfortable—you do it anyway.

You tell your friends I'll "rub them down" if they come over
You bring David by and he gets all excited thinking I'm going to fuck him … Whatever

I'm not your ho—
I don't do this shit. Out of my life fuck, mother fucker—that's it.

Gaining Weight

Again, here we go.
As of today I am on a diet, again.
Tired of the up and down.
I have gained twenty pounds in two months.
I need to lose it quick
Before I lose my mind.
I am working out on a regular basis still,
but because I am consumed with stress,
I have not been as good to myself as I should
Have been.
Go figure.
Once again, it is time to forget about others
And to worry about me.
Lose the weight,
Work more, sleep more,
Spend more time with me,
do my homework,
Get into my skinny jeans.

Gasoline

Poured all over my body
Burning pain frees my soul
Fire rips away my flesh
Making my being whole.

Gasoline penetrating my every pore
Soaking its way toward my core
Crying, dying, all done inside
Gasoline burns, puts out the fire

Rapes my innocence, frees my desire
Love is gone, burned in the crossfire
Heated grasp, you back away
Gasoline in my soul is here to stay.

Don't light a match near my indifference
You will lose me forever
Gasoline has my soul in shackles
How fucking clever.

Gasoline love
Gasoline hate,
I'm naked around you,
But it's too late

Body burned to the ground
You see right through my soul
I don't want to light
This fire anymore.

I see right through you
Gasoline
How does it feel
To be me?

Getting Fired

I got called into the manager's office today because
My "personal life has become a problem." Oh, right.
Is it because I do women and men? Oh my,
Let's all pull out the gun on this one, shoot her quick
Before she multiplies. I was warned that my personal life
Is never to be mentioned at work—again. The only reason
It was mentioned in the first place is because the other
Employees talk about their husbands, wives, kids,
And someone asked me about my love life … so I
Honestly said I haven't had a relationship in a while, but
The girl I was hanging with just moved out. And when guys
ask for my number I tell them, "I don't dig guys, but I am
flattered that you asked." So what if it isn't completely
True? It keeps their egos whole, and they leave me alone.
So anyway, someone told my manager that I
Was gay—and now I am an outcast
(Which by the way does not bother me at all)
But I can't afford to get fired because of my
Sexual preferences. So now I have to do the
One thing I am horrible at: lie. When people ask me,
I have to tell them, "Work is not the place to discuss
My personal life." Which is a great practice, if everyone
Follows it. Everywhere you go people talk about their
Relationships all the time. Damn, I am so frustrated.
People are constantly trying to suppress me. The more they try,
The more I want to scream and yell. What a crock of shit
That I have to deal with. I am way too open-minded; I hope
I can keep my mouth shut. It is hard to do: people ask,
And I don't have a problem telling them. Anyway,
Maybe one of my co-workers was right and I should make up
Some fake bullshit about how I don't date because I don't have
Time. Which to me is laughable because I make time
For my friends. But whatever; I will walk on
Eggshells and keep my mouth as shut as I can as often as I
Can so that I can keep my job, because inevitably it is
The most important thing right now, and as always, my
Happiness can wait. Still … there is a Christmas party
Coming up and family is invited, but my boss said it would be
Best if I came alone. Really? Didn't matter; got called in
By the head honcho, who fired me on the spot. Can't have that kind
Of reputation. Right. Oh, to hell with it. Fuck y'all.

Give Me Back

I am a puzzle of a million pieces
Everywhere I go I leave
Pieces of me
Some people stick around
Collecting pieces of my puzzle
Others decide quickly
I am not worth their time
Give back my piece
I'll reconnect
The picture reveals
The pieces of me
I love best.

Glacier

Frozen, like
Water from an icicle,
My blood slips, slowly, dripping
From the shapeless body once my life
Pique drips slowly from my pate to my feet
As I sip the salty tears that flow freely from
My soiled eyes.
The fiasco I see
This life that I try so hard to lead …
Glacier, frozen, my body free
My souls watch over as I melt
Ink-blue as water onto the paper I bleed
My words without notice
Take me, from me.

Glitter-Swept

Singled out on a vision of the word love
Its sharp letters fall from my lips
Only to break repeatedly into glittered pieces on my floor
You pick up the glitter,
Sprinkle it on your heart, wear it proudly—
As I cry tears of pain
For my heart you hold in pride.
Can I ask for the gentle return of my broken words?
Or do I need to walk away—
And say goodbye? Please—I beg of you—
I will not ask for my heart's return
But maybe you could loan me your letters,
Or money you could spare—so I can buy
More words to share, once again I've broken my heart.
The words fall from my lips—
I lie sparkling—beautifully—upon the floor
You sweep so heartlessly. Throw my pieces in the trash—
Walk away—I will love again another day
With or without my glitter, you so proudly let fall—
Upon your floor.

God

What do you see when you look into my world?
You see everything around—but do you see me?
I am the foundation of validity.
Without my presence, this magnificent creation
Would not be.
You can try to disregard me
But the lie will get you nowhere
My presence is key to life
In this secret somewhere
Never to be seen
I am the reason for this scene
I am God—
I am the reason behind the vision
Within the being.

God's Eyes on You

God's land saved—freed
Imprisoned you
Bitter lemon sadness,
Sweet Freedom soft upon my fingertips
Satin tears embrace my cheeks
Coldness grasps my inner being
Taken away from your zenith
Placed in someone else's solitude
Fear swallows the burdened heart
I hear you calling to me
Safety is what you seek
Pain is what you feel
Alone in someone else's mind
It is a pain that is all too real.
On God's land—you see yourself
Roaming high above the canopy
I break to you the reality of it
You are where we all long to be
Safe in another's world
Our sanity sets you free
In captivity you've been placed
But that is not what I see
The trees are your freedom
You don't understand
They placed you in a haven
This prison you call home
But they freed you from the bullet
Of the hunters who freely roam
They drew a circle around you
In order for you to be free
The forest may be the only thing
Keeping you from me
But the hunter knows your ways
And he too longs to be
On God's land
We are all imprisoned
Freedom is not free

God's Power will Succeed

I'm happy, I'm healthy, I'm wild, I'm fun.
I suck at relaxing, I'm pretty high strung.
Dangling from a tiny thread, my neck holds all my weight,
Loving the flavor of pain and the blood I create.
Long ago within my heart, I froze a special place,
A tender me, a loving being, one whom now I hate.
Broken I find my pieces, scattered upon the floor.
I seek them through wind and rain, as my soul pounds Satan's door
To me he crawls with questions, burning to know the truth.
"Are you broken because of God? Or are you broken because of you?"
With fire reflecting in my eyes, I lash out, filled with hate,
"Broken I am because of you! Don't placate.."
He laughs at my anger, he curses my name,
My fire is fed, but my ice will melt his flame.
As I turn to the door, I begin to retreat;
I take one look into evil's eyes and I see true defeat.
Not in his eyes, not in the reflection of myself,
But in the image in his eyes of God himself.
I feel God's hand upon my shoulder, hear words from heaven's wake,
Telling Satan, "You can't beat me. Get out of our way."
The game is broken for now, but I will once again be me.
God is on my side; right now, that is all I need.

Good Day Well Spent

A dime in a jar for everyday I've
Lived to the best of my ability.
To keep me strong—I want to be—
Well spent …

Goodbye My Sweet

I played with a deck of fifty-two cards
Came upon the unimagined:
A fifty-third. A Joker—what a find
I treasured that card like the trees drink the rain
In my hands, in my pocket: it never left my side
I smothered my Joker
Then one day it came time to play my hand
I knew my deck was special
The time came, my turn
Hand-to-hand, card to card—
She lay down an ace.
My joker went wild.

Got Checked Last Night

Same damn story—what was I thinking
They don't know any more than they did before I went in
I am going to be ok—it is all that I can be
Going through this so-called life, always just being me.
In a hurry to graduate, can't wait to teach.
Don't want to mess up any more; it's all that sets me free.
I am trying so hard to work on the issues of me, but
Every time I stand my ground, I get swept off my feet.
Well, not this time; it won't happen again.
I am going to go through life being alone and in pain.
I used to say it hurt too much to never know love at all,
But being alone at the hospital last night I realized,
Love hurts every time you fall. Being alone,
I'll never Falter …
I have loved plenty throughout my life, and yet I am still
Alone? In the hospital, cold.
My phone rang, familiar voice on the other end …
So unexpected … Made me want to cry … Wanted to be held,
I'll never know why. The person behind the voice knew right
Where to find me, knew something was wrong. I felt
So loved, so comforted, and yet so alone …
Damn, struggling, I am in pain, Pain of love, pain of self-reflection,
Pain of Endometriosis, pain of not being good enough …
I am alone, not lonely; I am in pain, not hurting;
I am scared, not afraid; I am in love, not loving.

Here We Go Again

Shit, here we go.
It's happening again …
Been with him for two months,
I am starting to fall … out.
I enjoy my time with him,
He is beautiful,
He is sweet,
He is caring,
He is patient,
He is everything I do not deserve …
I need to make him leave.
Only then will he see
He deserves so much more,
So much better than me.

Holding Onto Your Heart

I want to be the heat, the reason, the burning. I aim to
Complete the searches, find the reason to reach inside and
Make your cold heart burn. I want to take your ice
And make it drip to the core of you
I rip at the wall, at the flesh
Tear the veins to pieces, crack the ribs the sternum
Reach in and take your heart
Swallow it whole—no, better yet:
Place it under my pillow, hold it when I need it,
Caress it when it beats too fast, love it when it lets me,
Let it rest when it is calm, Put it back because I know
It does me no good to hold your heart if it is not within
You. Keep it cold if it means you hold me to you when you
Long for a warm heart.

How Hard

How hard is it to get happy;
How hard is it to just get into a good mood and stay there?
I wish I knew. I have been a ball of emotions lately.
I am afraid of messing up a good thing …
So much so that I am messing up a good thing!
I am trying so hard to be good. It is all I can do.
Smile and be happy and think about you.
I am trying so hard to do the right things in my life.
Getting rid of bad memories, eating right,
No more soda, trying to sleep right—I am doing better.
I just have to look at how far I've come,
Not taking things for granted. I am trying so hard.

Hypocrite

Funny how
"God bless us all"
Only works when it fits
Your standard of living.

It Hurts So Bad

I have to go to the hospital again;
I am in so much pain.
It's happening again, and I am uncomfortable.
My stomach …
My stomach.
I'm nauseated; it hurts to sit, it hurts to pee.
Damn it, the pain is really getting to me.
This is worse than the last time.
The last time was easy to deal,
It took weeks before I had to get help last time.
Now, I have to go today,
There's no way I will make it another day.
I have an important test tomorrow too;
I have to go today, nothing else will do.
It hurts so bad …
Can barely breathe,
Need relief.
How do I do this without my boy-toy finding out?
I have to be at the dentist at ten,
And with Cathy at half past noon'
I have to pick Adam up from school at four.
That gives me three hours to take care of this problem …
I hope I can do it.
Otherwise I'll have to go to the
Emergency room tonight,
And then the man would know for sure …
I am in so much pain.
Please, just make it go away …

<u>In the End</u>
Rear-ended lover
Walking away
Painful to find
Painful to play
Hit from behind
When you least expect it

Rear ended lover
Walking away
Hit and run
Couldn’t play the game
White back bumper
Red from the pain you left behind

Gotta look out for you
Next time I’ll do a better job
Pickin’ my ride—
I’ll buy a red one
So the pain I can hide
Behind the red paint
You leave behind.

I **<u>Am</u>**

Unusually unusual, how unusual of me
Predictably unpredictable, how unpredictable of me
Perfectly imperfect, how perfect of me.

I Am a Thief

In the night I do roam
Walking away
From the happiness
Of my so called home.

Tearing your heart
From the flag upon the pole
Stealing your dreams
Is my ultimate goal.

I will make you love me
I will stake my claim upon your soul
You will never be without me
Only together will you be whole.

I Am at Peace with a Dream Called You

You were a hope, a dream … and now you are not.
I was mistaken, but I have forgiven myself … forgotten.
No two visions are the same—the feelings will stay—
But the beauty behind them no longer remains.
I am so damn good at being alone.
It is insane—
I have forgotten to ridicule myself
For the way I felt about you.
I am not going to forget
And I am glad I got the chance
But that time in my life is over.
And I will forget.
I am at peace with a dream called you …
But that's not to say I never loved you.

I Am Beautiful

I am beautiful inside.
My body is borrowed and without it
I still have much soul.
I am worthy.

I Am Leaving

I am in a cold hell,
Ironic as it seems
Freedom in this place is a joke;
We sit here and laugh
At the passersby,
Say, "How do you do?"
They are so cold, so uninviting;
They just scowl at you.
One more year,
I swear it's true,
Oklahoma, I am coming home to you.
How things change:
It's November,
I am out of Massachusetts,
And I am struggling,
The people are nicer,
Life is better, and I,
I am exactly the same.

I Am Not Interested

I am not interested in talking if
You are not interested in talking …
Do me a favor—you want us
To talk? Start talking.

I Prowl

I am perfectly imperfect—how perfect of me.
Allow the tears to flow solemnly
Sweet child, woman wild
Sweet wild woman-child
Fear in the heart of the lover
Creates strength in the mind of the hunter
I hunt thee with fury … in my heart.

I Am Ready

I am in a race for survival
Taken to the grave through the struggle
For the pain in my feet and the rapid heartbeat
I lie down in my grave without trouble.

I Am the Rainbow

Black-eyed pearl
Diamond of blue
Share with me
The passions of you
Walk me into your prisms
Your rainbows of healing
Let me sparkle from your walls
Admit my hardened feelings.
Opaque dreams
Transparent lies
Let me hide these feelings
From the rainbow walls
Take my shadow's pride
Cold as ice my fire burns
Within the room the prism turns
Dancing with the sunlight
It is now that I see
I could never love you
For you cannot love me
So I'll take my frozen heart
And in my fire let it melt
Create the flames, burn what I've felt
Let the breeze carry the smoke into the sky
Cover the sun's golden rays forever
Clouds begin to cry
The rainbow has vanished—
And so have I.

I Am Tired

I am tired of all the bullshit
The fighting and the lies
I want to go back to Oklahoma
Where the weather is always nice
No more Massachusetts,
No more fucking black flies,
No more road-rage ignorant people
No more wanna-be good-byes.

I just want to leave this place
That rips my mind to shreds
Tiny little pieces falling
It's all that I have left
I have to pick up the pieces
Of what is left of my ripped up mind
I have to find some satisfaction
Before I lose it for real this time.

Manic-fucking-depressive
It's what you say you see
I see fucking obvious tension
Post-traumatic stress disorder
Couldn't diagnose me
Counseling psychologist:
It's what I aim to be
And once I have my licensure
I will diagnose me:

Happy, in Oklahoma.
That is the only label I want to see
No more unnecessary drugs
No more fucking fantasy
I will live in happiness,
Without the likes of you
Label this you son-of-bitch—
I've got better things to do.

I Don't Want Your Forever

Between you and I there is a very thin line.
You constantly toe the line on your side,
And me, I am constantly balancing on both sides.
Damn woman, I have a great idea.
Why don't we both wrap our arms around each other,
And two-step on the line?
Both of us can lead, both of us can follow.
Our line will technically never be crossed.
Because we will be always walking it together.
Until, that is, we walk away.
And that will have to be ok.
I don't want your forever.
I just want your today.
Want me the way I want you to …
Tomorrow is another day.

I Ended It

I am not perfect. I have some serious issues
I hate knowing that there are people out there that would do
Absolutely anything for me. I don't want people like that
In my life. I realize I am a hard person to live with but
I never cared before. Now I am starting to dislike my
Living arrangements, my job, and everything about myself.
This can't be happening again. I really don't know what to
Do when I get like this. Am I doomed to walk around this
way forever? Cycle this:
Love it so much I can't get enough of it,
Like it so much that one or two days without
Won't kill me,
Don't care one way or another …
Don't really want to see it at all
Don't want anything to do with it …
This is my life, and my life cycle so far …
I hope someday I will be able to change my stars but for
Now, I am burned out completely on love, Massachusetts,
And my job …
I need to rest.

I Hold You

I hold you within my thoughts
As I hold you within me.

I choose you,
I want to be your angel,
I want to be your shining star.
I want to be your glory,
Let me take you from where you are.

I need to be your soldier,
I want to be your hero true,
I need to be a loving friend—
Is that all right with you?

Let me be your sun-kissed clover,
Let me be a sinner,
Let me be a saint,
Let me run through your river,
Let me be your never wait.

I just want to hold you,
In hopes for the same
Hold me, as I hold you,
In my heart,
Forever.

I Know

Team meeting—I barely said one word
Four cups of coffee with pure sugar
I came home this morning acting a fool.
I overdramatized everything that came out of my mouth.
And I knew it—as soon as I drove out of my driveway.
I wanted so badly to take this morning back—all of it actually …
But I can't. I fucked up.
I don't like when I do that.
Maybe a day or two—alone—will be sufficient to get me back on track.
Maybe not. What do I know? I know I do not like me when I am like that.
But what else can I do? Apologize and move the fuck on.
But now I have lost credibility with them.
And how do I suppose I get that back?
Don't fucking do it again …
Whatever it takes, I guess.
I'm not perfect. I make mistakes …
I hope you know—because I know.

I Know a Man

I know a man
He is like a maze
Where the walls
Are constantly changing
And I love him anyway.

I know a man
He is like the dream
You never want to wake from
Because you might lose something
And I love him anyway.

I know a man
He is just like the soil
Beautifully nourishes, knows he is important,
Hides his pain through the splendors he creates
And I love him anyway.

I know a man
He walks like he is floating
He looks so nonchalant, so carefree
He carries the weight of the world on his shoulders.
And I love him anyway.

I know a man
He is just out of reach
The constant shadow dancing
On your bedroom wall when you wake up
And I love him anyway.

I Made Love

I made love to poetry last night,
And once I was done,
I lay naked by his side.
Thinking, remembering the smell of his skin,
The feel of his shaft penetrating deep within.
As he grabbed me from behind,
He lifted up my shirt,
I got onto my knees
And wiggled my ass
He laughed and he giggled,
He quickly dropped his pants.
Taking off my shirt,
Kissing the small of my back
I quickly turned him over,
And put my mouth over his rack.
Slowly, deeply, wetly, I sucked
As he moaned and he groaned
"Harder," he screamed
But I wanted to fuck.
I made love to poetry last night
He lay on his back
And I climbed on just right
His hands on my hips,
I gyrated and rocked,
He moaned and he groaned
And I simply pleased his cock.
Impatient and wet,
He turned me on my back
He grabbed my legs and spread them
Then went down for a snack
Making me moan
He grabbed both of my hands
He lapped and he hummed
And he laughed while he ate
Moving my lips from side to side
I could not wait.
I grabbed his arms with my nails,
And I pulled him to me
Shoving his shaft deep inside
He came instantly …
I made love to poetry last night.
He lays naked next to me this morning,
The light is just right,
And I know in my heart,
Poetry liked my rhyme.

<u>I Love the Sound of You</u>

I may be a simple drop of rain
Thrusting against your windowpane
But I'll take seeing you
Any way that I can.
Again, and again, and again
Rapping, tapping, pounding
Hard against the opaque glass
Which separates you from me.
I fall slowly, peering in
Upon your sleeping flesh,
Wanting, wishing, hoping
For our souls to mesh.
I may be a simple drop of rain
Thrusting against your windowpane
But I hold onto hope—
To see you once again.

If I <u>Live</u> to <u>Be One Hundred</u>

It will be 2079
What a reality check.
I wonder what the world will be like then?
Will there be marriage?
Will there be divorce?
Will there be children?
What am I thinking—of course …
There will be children—
But what will they be like?
Statistically—ninety percent of children born
In the years 2000-2003 were born
To children themselves,
Between eleven and fourteen years old.
What will it be in 2079?
How will my grandchildren live?
Will they be free?
Free to make their own decisions?
Free of pain and agony?
This is too much---
Too much for me—
I need to free my mind
Of these thoughts which consume me.

It's Raining

If it weren't for the rain,
I would feel nothing.
I am glad it is raining;
My mind is weary …
Alone alone alone.
Tomorrow, I will be
A beautiful flower.
Thank you rain.

I Hear Sweet Nothings

The person who sees only popularity
Becomes a mirrored image, reflecting whatever
Needs to be reflected in order to gain acceptance.
The person becomes everyone, and no one.
I will never be your mirror image. I am me.
I have made listening my best friend, and understanding
Has become best friends with me. That said, my mirror
Reflects understanding and the ability to listen
I hear the future calling, telling me sweet things.
Enticed by her sensuality, I move in closer to her sweet lips;
She turns my face with her cheek and whispers softly into my ear
Who knew the future was full of sweet nothings?
I guess I'll have to wait around and see just what
My future has in store for me …

Imprisonment

Cold and alone, shattered in two.
Fell for injustice
When I fell in love with you
Walking hand in hand,
I thought I could do no wrong
Then I saw you with another,
My evil demon spawned
Torn in two, ripped to shreds
Took out her heart, demolished her intent
Hatred, I have sent her
Sadness, I have given you.
You told me once you loved me
I believed it to be true
You settle for me, wanting her
I have walked away
No longer your keeper
Freedom you have found
Go forth and seek her
In this prison of love
Given evasive solitary
I will shelter myself forever
From the touch of any man
Knowing the pain you have caused me
Will only come again.

In a Mood

When things just aren't right
And there's nothing you can do
Do you walk away from it all?
Is there nothing else to do?

I am unsatisfied with my performance
I want a different job, different pay
I struggle with this twenty-four hours
Each and every day

I have things to show
For all the things I do
But damn, all I want to show for all I have
Is you

I struggle constantly with her in your life
Me as the lover, her as the wife
Eventually the roles may change
And she may be a small piece of your life

For now, I struggle
In a mood
I want everything and nothing
Most importantly, I want you.

In Love

All love is not lost as long as you are a part of me.
In this world I conquer the forest and its trees,
The lush green waters flowing, the birds who sing to thee
I create a new habitat, a safety for me and you.
Evil has taken over, but I will fight its demons with you.
As your knight in shining armor, and your tributary with
Shield in hand, forever in your honor I fight, forever I take the stand.
My princess, I hold your honor above all others
Thy admiration true. Love me as you've loved no other;
I vow to always protect you.

In the Dark

In the dark of night I suffer
From the vision that lies not
Within the room, but within myself …

In the Fire

The fire
Lit and moving
Has been tested
My life is
Cold as ice
My water,
In solid form,
Has challenged the fire.
Is it strong enough
To put it out?
I guess we will have to wait and see …

In This World

In this dog-eat-dog world
I am a dog.
I have eaten with the best of them,
And I have been eaten by the best of them.
But I always seem to heal,
And get back up there with the rest of the best of
Them.

Indifference

Indifference
Toward
You in
Your world
Of blue
Screen
Graphics
Known you
For some time now
And I have to say
I do not miss you
Not in the slightest
Do not call me
And I will not
Call you
I do not miss
Your indifferent
Attitude
Toward
Me
I do love you
But I love you
More
From a distance
Greater than
You
Or I
Can create.

Innocence as Spellbinding as the Eyes of a Tiger

I showed no shame
And now I see
That I loved you
More than endlessly

Innocent

Innocent cow
Hunts aimlessly
For her sanity
Through the grass
She searches
For her unfeeling indifference.
Stops by the stream of conundrum—
Oxymoronic thought—
If only she could masturbate her intellect like me …
She would find her sanity—for sure.

Intense

I want to hold you
To taste your kiss
To feel you close to me
I long to rub your back with my finger tips
To lay naked by your side
To smell you
To be consumed by you.

Interpretation

What in the world are the birds doing here?
They flock and they sing and they bring music to my ear
But what of their song they want us to hear?
Where is the sadness that falls through the tears?

Intertwined

On her stomach she sleeps in a satin blue gown.
Her hair flowing softly, on her breast, all around.
He slips into the room like an owl in the night,
Seeking his prey when the moment is right.
Laying his head upon her back, trying to wake her,
He holds tightly to her body, dare not forsake her.
Longing to be within her, her passionate undress
He slips himself inside her for a moment. She is tense
With a struggle, then a sigh, she lets herself free,
He allows himself to take charge, moving rhythmically.
Inside and out, deep and then low,
Gently pleasing her body, moving to her moans.
Making love to the moment, him inside of her,
Together they orgasm; he holds her through her quiver
Loving the feeling, together, he falls asleep inside of her,
Like a melon to a vine, incomplete, complete, intertwined.

Irony of the White Lie

Do not burn me with your lies; they are not worth being called "white"
White
Alludes to innocence
Lies
Are not white
Lies
Burn within us
Blackness
Torn pain through smoke filled lungs.
Lies
Pain can be saved for words spoken—without truth.
Lies
Eventually will be put to fire
Lies
Create the guilt, which burns behind the need for truth.
Lies
Engulfed in flame torn to many truths.
Honesty
The largest fire
Burning
With creativity
Laughing
At your indifference.

Killing the Demon

I killed my inner soul,
To be re-born again.
The best thing,
I have done for myself.
Schizophrenic lover
Within my heartbeats
My existence will reign
For my mind to defeat!

It's So Easy

It's so easy to forget about me
When I'm not around.
Don't fuck with my head; I'd
Like to keep my heart inside of me
And off the ground.
Walking around, bewildered at your interest in me.
I don't understand it—
I guess I just can't see.
What it is you want from me?
I haven't told you what I am,
So why do you see me as worthy?
Can I have your hand please?
I want to feel you breathe again,
The way you did when I placed my hand
Upon your cheek.
It's ok if it is a temporary fix.
I don't need you to want me forever
I just want you to want me for the moment.
Sad, but true—
I could never be enough for you.
Yeah we'd be great together …
But I have this problem with commitment—
And no, it's not because I am afraid to get hurt;
It is because I am afraid the passion will die
And it will be my fault.
I am moody
And I am creative—never a good combination.
You keep saying "I should grab it while I can"—
Do you mean you want me?
Are you fucking with my head?
I guess I would give you the chance,
But I just don't understand.
We would be awesome lovers
(You were right about that)
But if that is good—is that that?
If that that is that is that and that that is not is not
That then is that it?

It Won't Go Away

It's so difficult to see you right now.
Girl, I could love you the way you want me to.
I could care about you the way no one else could
I could be there to care when no one else would.
I could stand your test of time.
I could make love to your intellect.
I could please you with my mind.
What is standing in the way?
I do not want to hurt you.
I don't like that you see me as a player,
That you don't see past my façade,
That you can't get to know me any better than that.
I don't want you to love me if it's not what you want.
I can get over the way I feel, the wanting you around.
The longing for your voice on the phone;
I can get over the incessant need of wanting to hold you.
I can get over wanting to be part of your life;
And once I do, I will forever be a part of you.
I know how you feel, baby, I see it in your eyes,
I feel it from your smile. I know you could love me
It's a feeling too hard to hide, to deny,
Although I know how hard you try.
But I know you can't—and trust me, I know why.
You have to do what's right for your family,
Do what's right for you.
Forget about me and this will come more easily.
Do what makes everyone else happy;
Dismiss the thoughts of me and you.
Don't think no one else will notice
When you sit down to call
The look on your face when your heart falls
And you have to put the phone down and walk away
Because you are afraid of what everyone else might hear you say.

Easy to Fall

I may be, as you all say, easy to fall in love with,
But I am, as I have proven, hard to *stay* in love with.
Fall if you must; it won't get you anywhere but hurt.

Jimmy Rigged

Addicted to the chaos
You like being the victim of the game
Taken from your element
You leave your friends behind
So that they don't see
This chaotic love that you invite
The abuse that sets you free
You hang your head in shame
When your friends are around to see
But they are none the wiser—
They are victims of this game of love
That sets your passions free
You find chaotic love,
And you become intertwined
Loving every minute of what you find.
Your friends will stand beside you
Holding your hand as you allow
But the only time you'll come around
Is when the abuse begins to show through
You latch on where you can
It makes you feel like you are worthy
No one else will ever understand
Pushing your friends away.
How long can you do this to yourself?
Holding on for one more day
You latched onto me as soon as
You realized my days are filled with chaos
I lead a crazy life
Then you figured out
That maybe you should see
Just how fucking chaotic a life you could lead.
And when you start to realize
That all of your friends can see
That you are keeping the chaos around …
It is then that you set them free.

Kids

Question authority, democracy, literacy, algebraic equations.
But don't just accept an answer, accept an answer with an explanation!
Want to know? Need to know? Can't have the Kool-Aid without the sugar …
Why? One way too tart, one way too sweet; powder plus sugar becomes complete
Make a statement, set curiosity free, allow yourself to understand
All you can be. You must question everything …
Identity will be figured out once questions begin flowing.

Just Believe

I promise myself today: I will not call you again.
Write myself a note, no more trying.
    God has a plan for me—and it does not include you
    I know this for a fact
I know this to be true
    It is a beautiful day
    It's supposed to get nicer
Let God lead the way
Make the most of what you have
You are going places
You will someday. You are a one of a kind,
Child of love. Forgive through God.
    Let God take your anxieties, let him take away your pain,
    Help him create within you—be all that you can.
You are worth it. Know this to be true.
No one but you and God can change these things in you.

Just to Be Where I Can Be Me

Born into a world
Where people are cruel
Sitting all alone, pain envelops you.
Crawl into a hole
Feeling unsure of what to do
Crying—dying—burning inside
Fuel for the fire, trying to hide.
Run deep into the forest
Sure never to be found
Feel the beauty of the surroundings
Red-breasted robin singing in the trees
Maples and pines, swaying with the breeze.
Lost in the beauty of the effervescent skies.
No longer needing to run
No longing to hide
Capable of finding beauty
Within the cruelty of the world
Sit within your solitude
Pain no longer heard, lonely in repression
Crying you no longer need to do
Not because you are not sad.
But because no one will hear you …

Last Day of Class

Everyone sitting, pondering what their grades will be
Sitting, hoping for an A or a B,
Worrying, wondering, studying, struggling—fear
Ten after nine, wondering when you will get here,
Not knowing what to think. You walk in the door,
The tension is released—and yet, increased …
Journal entry: AAA … Do it right, get an A;
Learned a lot, walk away. Thank you.

Last Night Ended in a Lie

Something got me locked up last night. I know what it was.
I'll never say. It won't matter anyway. It was stupid, and even petty.
He and I are doing well right now. A little too well…
I started thinking things I shouldn't. Acting in my mind like I am ready,
Feeling just a little too sure of myself, I tried to play it off. It worked, but I wish I could have just been honest.
I enjoy my time with him; he's not complaining much.
I still act so insecure around him …
It's just an act; I'm not really that trite. It's crazy the way I do that
So that I don't have to open up. With everyone else I walk with my head held high …
With him, I guess I just don't trust us fully.
There's not really any reason for it,
But I feel like if I act self-conscious he'll get sick of it and leave.
The truly sick thing is, I don't want him to, not at all.
I could be with him forever.
And I would even be willing to give him the ring
The ceremony, the certificate—I know how important it is to him.
I would wear the ring proudly. I can't say much for the rest of it,
Because I am still not sure what it is all for.
But if it reassures him that I will never leave,
Then he will get what he wants. I still have my moments though …
You know the ones. "He's just like every other guy;
He'll fuck you and leave—just wait, you'll see,
He must have a few tricks up his sleeve." I wish
I wouldn't do that, I wish I could just believe.
But he is human, and he will make mistakes,
And I will forgive him, if that's what it takes.
I am strong enough to walk away, but I don't think I will.
He means so much to me already that I know how leaving him would feel.
It's part of the reason I haven't done it. I couldn't if I tried. I said it before, this is beyond me.
I am not in control of this relationship, and I won't try to be.
I know that if he were to get caught in a lie,
Even cheating, it would really mess with me. But I also know,
I've been there before, and it would not be the death of me.
I didn't cry when another left, or when he cheated on me.
But I remember how much it hurt, and how much I blamed me.
I felt like I couldn't do anything right,
But I'm much smarter than that now; if I am with
Someone who cheats, I know it proves that I am strong,
And they are truly weak.
I can walk away from temptation—I do it every day.
He seems like he can too, but I see the capability in him.
We all have it, but what would we do?
He has cheated before, which means he could revert,
But I have not, and I know why; I know how much it hurts.
I have a lifetime to prove to him that I don't need to hurt him.
I am willing to give him my time, because I know
How good he is for me. I just need to be stronger around him.
Stop playing the scared little girl, because this act, it isn't me,
And I'm tired of acting hurt. The other guys, they are in the past,
And I have let them go. He is my present, and
If he'll stick around to see, he'll be my future, forever more.
I lied last night, to the man I love,
Not to save his feelings, but to act unnerved.
He'll never know, so I will never see what it is he wants to do,
Me loving him, him loving me.

Amanda Suddeth

Everyone Else

It's so easy to forget about me when I am not around.
Don't fuck with my head;
I'd like to keep my heart inside of me
And off of the ground.
Walking around bewildered at your interest in me.
I don't understand it—
I guess I just can't see, what it is you want—
What do you want from me?
I haven't told you what I am not worth,
So why do you see me as worthy?
Can I have your hand please?
I want to feel you breathe again
The way you did when I placed my hand upon your cheek.
It is ok if it is a temporary fix.
I don't need you to want me forever,
I just want you to want me for the moment.
Sad, but true.
I could never be enough for you.
I have this problem with commitment.
And no, it is not because I am afraid to get hurt;
It is because I am afraid the passion will die.

Lies

Lies break the barriers
Of all foundations

Liar of Truth

You tell me one thing … You tell them another.
Story of my life. I am in the dark world of your heart—
The one you keep so fucking secret.
Are you taking this personally? You should …
        And you … And you … And you …
Each and every one of you.
You love me, as long as you can keep me at a distance.
You never tell: your wives, your husbands, your best friends,
Even when your best friend is me …
        You all fight so hard to keep me secret.
Why me? Why do I have to be your secret?
I am tired of the shoulda, coulda, woulda.
You are all so fucking scared. What have I done?
        Are you afraid of the ridicule you might receive for being with me?
Why am I the one? The one you love truly but could never be with?
The one who completes you so much you run away
No one will ever know the sacred place
I hold in your heart. I only know what you tell me
        Before the finality of the day. You walk away,
Toward the one you love, slowly releasing my hand …
And I simply stand alone. You don't understand how I have no one,
And still, I am not lonely … You have her, and yet, you call me to confide,
        You call me to cry, you call me when she's ripping you up inside.
I am your secret, your lover by heart. I will always be your best friend …
Your counselor.
But I will not let you own me.
I will remain your secret
        And no one else will ever know, but when you take your heart away—
Only your pain will show a secret shadow, and I will dance away …
No pain to show, no secret displayed.
Into someone else's arms I will fall today, and when you wake
You will smell my secret, feel my truth.
        A secret I will become to them, a regret I'll be to you.
Do you see my face when you are making love to her?
        Do you lick the sweet syrup of my kiss from her lips?
Tell me, do you wake in the night, anxious,
        Reaching for me—holding her?
I bet you do.

Little One

When your little girl is sick
What will you do?
Will you walk away afraid?
Or hold her close to you?

When your little girl gets bigger
And it's time for you to leave
Will you love her in fear?
Or keep her young as you believe?

When your little girl says,
"I don't want you here,"
What will you say?
What will you feel?

When your little girl is all grown up,
No longer needs you through the day,
Will you let her live with freedom
Or will you, angry, walk away?

When you need your little girl
Will you let her see your sickness?
Will you let her feel your fear?
Will you know she'll hold you close?

Little to None

Gotta get this right
Not much time you know,
Working on my life
These feelings flow.
Right through me—and onto you …
The sweat drips from my pores and seeps into you.
What's left within me I can't sweat out,
You wonder why I'm cold—
But you can't find it in you to take on my cold heart.
Little to none—my sweat drips
From my pores, my soul is ripped—leaving me cold—
That's what it is intended to do
Drying me out—my soul becomes you.
And you finally see what you love about me.
No hope—I mean little to none—Black is here, and white is gone.
I have nothing to give you, my soul is gone—
My heart remaining … and I am drained.

Love Is

Love is a sour rose given beauty through color's redress
    Red, yellow, white, pink …
Love is a beautiful rose given death through plucking
    Black …
Love is taken for granted, losing one's self, lacking conversation
    A rainbow of color …
Love is excruciatingly painful.

Love Truly

I know I have to let you go.
It doesn't hurt—
Wait, let me take that back.
This is hurting you, not me.
You are so caught up in how you think I feel,
Want me to feel, wish I would feel
That you can't see how I
Feel at all.
I've walked away from situations like this
A million times. Piece of cake.
This is not the end for me.
It is a whole new beginning.
But you see, that's where
The true problem lies.
Don't worry. I'll walk away—
It's easier on you both that way.
You'll see. Because I love you,
Truly. One day you will see …
When I am gone
Completely.

Making Love

Lost in the fog, naked, passionate,
Fighting these emotions,.
And the white water rides the black forever,
As I drown within the rock.
I crack its soul, break its emotionless keep.
I become one with its life.
From within the pebble I create—
New life I find through me
And the broken rock sits—
Cracked in a river of my love,
And the white water rode the black forever.

Man

Sadness breathes in the eyes of creativity
I see all
Laughter seeps through the heart of
The demon with your name
Grab hold of
The time I share with you.
What you do
Killing me
I love you.

Manic-Depression

Take my heart
But do not break it
Do not promise to hold onto it forever
Your hands will get tired
Do not attempt to play with it
It will grow cold and stop palpitating
Take my eyes
But not their passion
Do not stare into them
They will not tell you stories
Do not expect them
They cannot give you much.
Take my tears
But do not laugh at them
Your fingers will get wet
Do not ignore them
They need to be recognized
You will drink
Take my soul
But do not lose it
Do not fill your days with me
You will die of insomnia
Do not fill your nights with me
You will never want to wake
Take a little piece of me
But do not take just that
Do not stop taking pieces
Pick them randomly and fair
Do not judge me by those pieces
I have love everywhere
Take my evil
But do not let it scare you
Do not sell me short
I have goodness to spare
Do not forget to give it back
I do not wish to share
Take my goodness
But do not take it far
Do not let it get to you
I need my only charm
Do not let the world see it
My weakness is wide
Take my love for you
But do not keep it in a jar
Do not fear my solitude
In this I have advanced
Do not fear my attention
You are my waking star

Amanda Suddeth

Media

So good for sucking the marrow out of the bone
So much for the good, the negative sells
The promise of power in the painting of a man
Vision of submissiveness in the woman, drawn by a man's hand
Do men continue to be objects of heroism?
Do women continue to sell themselves for attention?
Face covered in duct tape the woman speaks
Child tied to a chair, silenced, tells all
The color of peace united … divided.
The person in the mirror, false truth
Images of media: truest form of lies
Sadness within poetry—media porn …
Without media in our faces, passion dies.
Emotions torn, children cry. Images reborn.

Messed Up

At your
Indignation
I smile
At your pain
Because it
Is all I can do
You laugh
At my happiness
Trying to make
Me feel you
But I cannot
And therefore
Will not
And so
I leave
Satisfied

Mind-Fuck

Rancid fingertips rub my solid nipples
Bring my skin to tears,
Make my flesh sparkle
Yearning to touch your naked body.
Lay down beside me.
Holding you, tasting you.
Showing you what it's like,
What I can do.
Different than most—stimulate your intellect.
Never have to see you naked.
Knowing I make you cream.
The smile on your face and the glow of your skin
Gives away the wetness you try to hide from me
Someday maybe you will see
What great fuck buddies we could be
Devour my lips, make my body scream
Touch my emotions with your fingertips—
Absolutely free.
Heat from your body. Makes me numb
Tempting—we'll see.

Misplaced Inspiration

The beauty of the fall leaves
Red, green, yellow, orange, and brown
The smell of the cold as it brushes your face.
Halloween, costumes, candy, and children.
Coats, and gloves, sweatshirts, pants, and boots.

The beauty of the snow.
Covered trees—white, cold, and beautiful.
The chill of the snow as it touches your nose.
A warm cup of cocoa.
Chocolate, marshmallows, creamy warmth.

The beauty of inspiration.
Christmas lights aglow, children playing in the snow.
Cookies on a table by the warmth of a fire.
Being with loved ones,
A feeling beyond mention.

These are the things I miss most.
When the ground is dry,
The temperature high
And inspiration nowhere to be found.

Mistaken Emotion

Head tripping, drunk from the intellectual orgasm
Which you force upon me from behind.
Different from all the others, you made sure to ask my permission—
Even though you never cared if I gave it.
It was too late. The mind-fuck was so good we were not going to stop.
Never touching, yet the fingers of your mind probe my inner self
And make me breathless. The excitement intensifies
You realize we are on the same page, reading from our self-written erotica.
You graze my heart, notice like your fingers, it is cold as ice.
Frozen by cold hearted bastards.
Breathing their lies into me
With the grace of their tongue upon my lips.
Guarded, my frozen heart begins to beat
From the warmth of your flesh upon my soul.
This new warmth intrigues you, and still abruptly you retreat,
Knowing in your mind that this sudden pulse
Is not yours to touch.
The game becomes real as you see the fire within
Shine through my eyes, flashing images of those who've
Come before you in hopes of releasing my frozen heart for a time.
Wanting more, but knowing better, you realize I am the game,
And the fire will win.
My heart will freeze and I will be dead to you again.
I showed you my passion, and frightened, you ran away.
Beautiful, real, I will never be,
Good enough for you.
You are way too good for me.

Mother Daughter Mother

I am an astonishing caterpillar
I will never jump, run, or feel the breeze on my face.
But I will conquer all
I know I can manage, crawling to you
I will eat your leaves with love,
I will sleep upon your ground without remorse
Creature of beauty will someday be free
To fly within the low-lying clouds,
To dance in the wind,
Most of all to roam
With the other beautiful creatures
I will someday fly in heaven's wake
Until then, I perch with the other
Caterpillars here on Earth
Mother
I may be your
Daughter
But I will soon be
Worthy of being
Mother.

Music as Media

The silence took over a room filled with inquiring minds
Enquiring the hidden meaning of the heard, but never listened to words.
Like ink into the concrete the meaning envelops our beings
"And the people bowed and prayed to the neon god they made."
And they wondered at the truth behind the minute shivers evoked within.
"And the sign flashed out its warning, in the words that it was forming."
And all at once they knew why it was their skin was crawling.
They began to wonder at the life they led, if it really had true meaning
"Think you own whatever land you land on."
And what if we believe that "the earth is just a dead thing you can claim."
Do you start to question your self worth, and the goodness you sustain?
When your skin stops crawling and the ink within you disappears
You realize it starts again. "Sometimes you'll be held up,
Sometimes held down …" And you know, "You got to cry a little, die a little."
To know what it is you are living for, fighting for—otherwise,
"Suicide, it's a suicide, yeah."
Did you listen to the words that time?

My Friend

Never around when I need her.
Anxiety attack for two days straight.
Couldn't sleep, couldn't eat.
Got no one.
Where is my friend when I need her?
Never here.

My New Journey

I have a new roommate. He's cute, and sweet, everything a
Woman would want, everything I don't deserve.
We talk every day, for hours, on the phone and in person.
He will make a good roommate. (And he's a clean freak—
Bonus!) He told me he predicts that we will be together
Someday; I told him he sounds like everyone else in my
Life. He kissed me, and told me he had a lifetime to prove
It to me.
He is playing me a song right now, one
He called my song. He's a smooth operator,
But I know his kind. He'll get
Laid, and go away;
It's just a bunch of child's play.
I went to church today,
I was uncomfortable.
I went with a friend.
She was really worried about me.
I lost control and my tears fell.
We drove around and listened to some good music;
She hugged me, she kissed my forehead.
She asked me why I was crying, and I told her the truth.
I've never been good enough;
God won't want me around either.
She grabbed me and told me
She wished I did not feel that
Way, but that she knew I felt it was real
Within me, and she's right.

My Salvation

Everybody is so damn sure that I am a cold-hearted
Bitch who lies all the time, and yet it is
Funny: those who believe that
Must not know me at all. I made love
To her; I love her, always, but so what … and I
Fuck him, and I will never love him—half the time I
Cannot stand him, but so what … I don't have time for
Settling down. I am not really good at that anyway.
I told her not to call me again. I went to his house
To make it clear that I was not staying.
It's no surprise to me that he has not called.
I do not need bad energy at all in my life.
I went out with this guy
The other day who tried to force himself on me …
Good thing that nothing came of that.
Whatever … I am sad no longer; filled that space
With anger … I will be ok. Need to go for a walk.
I will be good enough someday.
Until then, I will continue to use my body as my toy,
My weapon,
My salvation.

My Secret

My secret garden of turmoil.
Riddled with flowers from beyond.
Captivated not by their beauty
But by their thorns.
Drowning in the soiled mess
From which they plant their roots.
I am falling out of me, and
Desperately into you.
Lightning rides the rain,
My responsibilities haunt my dreams
Rape my mending brain.
I cry tears of loneliness deep within,
Where no one else can see.
I long to bury my face in the mud,
And replant this seed of joy
My branches are long and withered,
My tree of life has died.
I am full of lapsed responsibilities and lies—
Failure is my lot.
I will never be good enough for you,
My roots keep my truth, and so I hide
Within the walls
Of shame. I wear my long face.
You will never see these feelings,
And I will never tell.

Amanda Suddeth

My Spinning Head

Spinning, spinning
My head is consistently spinning
I am ready to walk away
From the pain which consumes
My life

Straighten up.
You have a lot to learn
Stressed out, the tables will turn
Walk away baby—
Take care of you

I am here—not walking away
I am here—here to stay.
Sadness breathes through the
Eyes of
Captivity

My Thoughts

My thoughts are random,
Incriminating. I wish I did not think so much.
I would be so much happier.
The fear and frustration I carry with me
Comes not from my choices
But from the idea that I do not want to die
The way I have lived …
My ideas, my philosophies, my opinions,
Even my day-to-day struggles,
Are filled with bitter depictions of this world
That these scholarly fucks cannot fathom,
And I am sick of fighting the current.
I am ready to walk away from the bullshit,
To prove that I am worth more than these people presumed,
I have a greater sense of self.
I have you, but you are not mine to keep.
You are here by your own accord, and can leave
Whenever you feel my anger, stress, and fears are too much.
But I do have a greater role than I have ever realized …
I am a woman.
I am frustrated that I have no control over
The things in my life that I cherish the most …
Until I do, I will continue to work too much,
Stress about the less important things in life,
And try my hardest to show you how much
You truly are appreciated.

Need to Be

When will I come down
From this rain cloud so high?
Falling to the
Ground is a
Feeling of release …
A feeling of
Intense loss in which I
Need to mislay my self-control.
To get lost in
Losing-tomorrow
Is where I need to be.

Nevermore

I am done with the chaotic detour
Always find my way back
Nevermore.

I am tired of being the whore
Encapsulate my demons—find their pain
Nevermore.

I am filtered, I am trite, I am random
Change these things—never happy
Nevermore.

I am handcuffed to time, tied down to fate
Although I know better
Nevermore.

Never Identifying That Anything Is Wrong Means Never Fixing It

The larger scope of things looked at and never seen
You hear with your eyes open and your ears see everything.
Read the numbers, add the words, drive the car, confusion turns.

Stand back and breathe, open your eyes, envelop everything.
Start over, read with your eyes, listen with your ears, envision …
Futuristic—Detailed—Oxymoron—Holistic—Mechanistic—Oxymoronic

New to Me

I'm new to belief
I am trying so hard to understand,
And tragically, I am failing.
        I'm sure some people would not agree,
        But to me, it is all so confusing.
        The scriptures, the traditions, wrong and right.
I just don't know if I will ever get it.
I went to church last night to pray.
I needed to badly—rough couple of days.
        I went to the prayer room,
        Told God my fears,
        Someone was listening ...
And she replied. I am glad she did,
Her words calmed me, and so I didn't mind.
        She said, "The next time you give something to God,
        Turn around and walk away
        Picture yourself face to face with God,
        Handing him your troubles.
        Now, picture yourself snatching it back.
        Do you really think you could? I doubt you do."
Trying too hard:
It's what I am good at;
Really, it's what I do.
        I went to my church Sunday mornings,
        I went to church with my ex,
        I never felt comfortable.
I tried to pretend my church was working,
But the girls were just so tough on me, (in my mind);
AT his church, no one said a word (they must just not like me)
        All this learning I still have to do,
        Struggling with insecurities:
        God will never love me; how could he? I will never do.
I am wrong, and I know that is true.
My girls were trying to be helpful;
At his church, well, I never really tried to talk to anyone.
        All along it's been me,
        My fear of not being loved.
        God, Christianity, just another step up.
For years I denied the Lord:
What if he doesn't love me,
If I'm not good enough?
        How can I live by the Bible if I don't understand it?
        How can what it says be true, if one Christian does a thing,
        Another Christian would never do?
Pre-marital sex, wedding ceremonies, abortions,
Spousal abuse, divorce, drugs and alcohol ...
This religion stuff is confusing.

No Good Reason

We are fucking ourselves up and
There is no reason for it.
In love, you're cold, you're scared.
One minute you love the
Thought of being with me—
The next you can't stand it.
One second you look at me
Through rose-colored glasses—
The next with a blindfold on.
I tell you honestly when I want
You. But I fail to mention when I don't.
Maybe I should have told you when
I was simply fucking you and
Did not want to try to decipher from your
Fingertips if you were making love.
My heart bleeds every time you mention
That you might leave. My, I, me—we
Are not ready for that. I enjoy
Having you around too much.
But leave if you must. I understand.
What you need to know—
If you leave, I will still be your friend.
I will still do for you as you need me to.
Stop worrying that I expect
Anything from you. Maybe my words
Are too much. Maybe I need to show you
With my touch—or lack thereof.
Body language speaks so well;
Holding you is only one hour
Away … for now anyway.
Try if you'd like, but you will see.
I will never let you forget;
Therefore you'll never forget me.

Not in the Mood

Walk away now
Just let me go
Not in the mood for the bullshit
That goes along with
Going along with
You.
Maybe that's my truth
You'll never know
You're not strong enough to stay
So I will watch you go.

No Story Worth Telling

I have no story simply because my life's
Battle is meager compared to most.
In my mind, I am the only one who can
Surrender to this turmoil within, so
Burdening other people with it seems
Silly and almost selfish. But since you asked,
I will not be rude and
Disregard … I don't talk to many
People about this, and
It's not easy to tell. I have an issue with
Attachment. I do not allow
People to get close to me.
I will be happy, passionate, joking, and
Loving at one moment, but
Once I realize that the person
For whom I am on fire
Starts to get close, I
Shut down, freeze up.
No smiles, very cynical, extremely bitter.
I do it to keep people out,
Not because I fear getting hurt,
But because I have mastered the art
Of keeping people just out of
Reach. Most people stick around when
I am on fire, and leave once my ice returns.
Thus far in my life, attachment to most things,
Including God,
Has been my biggest
Battle.

Not

Not incompetent
Not in control
Not in love
Not in lust
Not anymore

Not Working

I am distant,
I am mean;
Still he cherishes me.
I guess I have to give up this fight
He is here for the long haul
And truly, I hope he stays.
I can see myself with him
Five years from now
It seems to fit
It's been a long time since
I have felt this way
And I do not want to give this up
Maybe I should challenge myself
In a new direction for once
Maybe the challenge should be
If I can keep him around
Maybe I'll prove I am good enough?

Note to Self

I need to grow wings
My anxieties own me
I must run

Oh, poetess, scared to write?
Scared to love?
Do not challenge your worth.

I know what you need
The ravishing sunlight on your face
Easing your heart

Stop worrying—please
Take control of your emotions—
Worry about your own needs

Take care of yourself
Make the day shorter, work hard
Loving me—Loving you.

Numb

Numb to the point I could pass out.
Saying goodbye: not for me; I am too strong for that.
Wait and see. I'm not crying, not trying to be willful
Think I'm beautiful
I can hardly stand to see
Why my beauty is only skin-deep
Sad but true—can't you feel
My beauty is found within you.
I am only as pretty as you allow me to be
As the yellow rose sits back to sing
I am not beautiful if no one admires me.

Observation

Voice—deep and lonely
Calling to you into the night
Dark bedroom swallows me
Blankets suffocate

Window opens
Enchanting breeze caresses the room
I cry—holding my pillow tightly
Soft velvet darkness—teasing my fear—teasing me.

Depressing, like clouds on a sun-kissed day—taken over
Killing me, a glowing orb just above the horizon
Knowing I must face
Another day—

Blue eyes staring through the mirror
Yours—fear envelops my soul
Beautiful chaos, lifeless
I gaze into the emptiness

Behind your sapphire stare—stone
Masturbation of matured souls, dying
Fingering through the emotions
Diving creation, calling you

I surrender to the pain—your pain
I long to walk away, captivated by the image
The happiness I hold derives
From passionate hell—I surrender

To this satanic touch
Emotional recreation
You, I realize now
Never existed

Close my eyes
Saunter in the opposite direction
Of your dead heart
Freedom found …

On a Mission

On a mission
To make things right

I will not walk away
I would rather fight

Until the end
Through tomorrow

I'll take control,
The ultimate defeat

Fuck you
For fucking me

You'll get yours
You'll see

You'll never know
What hit you …

But I will.

On My Journal

I like things the way they are.
Not sure I want anything to change.
I need to do some growing up
Before my emotions fade.
I like my jobs, but I'm not trying
As hard as I could to keep them.
I am not very proud of me at the moment.
Not sure what to do about all of this.
I have very few worries, and not many complaints.
I guess my thoughts just need releasing
So I can be true to me—to you.
I don't mind always writing—
It allows me to be honest in all I do,
But sometimes I just wish
I had someone to confide in—
Someone other than you.

One Try

I'm willing to give this one try
Do not fuck this up.
Unless that's what you want
But if so—
That doesn't seem right.
Why would anyone start something good
Just to go and fuck it up?
I'm not into all the nonsense
That revolves around relationships.
It's not for me.
I am giving you a shot—
Trusting
Which is one thing I am not good at.
But I guess we'll have to see
Where this will go,
Where it will lead.
I've got nothing better to do
Stopping me
Loving you
Not yet
But I'm willing to give it one try.

O Confused One

I love you, girl, you just don't know.
You think I talk to everyone the way
I talk to you; how do I explain
That is not true? I wish you could see,
How great it would be … I will
Never get the chance, so, fine:
I will be your best friend for
As long as you'll let me. But I
Want you to know, if you tell me to
Pack up my shit, and sell what
I can, you might have me for a while,
I might be a part of your plan.
You name it, time and date, I am yours …
Until then, I wait. Straight girl
Fights a battle within, I
Am the demon, and I will win.

Open My Heart

I posses my mind. The days are long and intertwined.
I walk away from the thing I cherish and leave the past behind.

Toward a new day; the sun is rising
I follow the beauty of the quickly changing horizon
Reach for the day that stands before me
Longing for God to be waiting for me.

Look back as the sun begins to descend, to vanish
Feelings fall with the dark and banish
Sadness dies with the beauty behind the day
Keep my eyes forward—stand and walk away.

The moon is deep; the night is dark; out of reach and cold
A symbol of my heart, steeped in sadness, getting old
The beauty of the night remains untouchable
The love and all romanticism, unreachable.

I want what I give, so I'll never be satisfied
I long for someone to understand that I have tried
I wait for him to come along, the feelings to be true
The moon will set, the sun will rise, and I will eventually find you.

Over It

This has been real tough for me
Cut off—no chance for survival
The only other guy who's ever done that to me—doesn't matter.
But you—you are no different than the rest,
And yet, I long to hear your voice—
To see you smile—to feel you naked—close to me.
You lied, you stole, you cheated, you disguised you
The *mask* you wear in your everyday life will leave
A vulnerable impression upon everyone you *face*.
You tried to use my words against me—fool
You said you were leaving, started packing your things, decided not to go
Two days later, I told you to leave, and when you left … you blamed me—
What a wicked game you play.
I guess you are just sharing your weakness in that way
One day you will see, I am not for you, and you are not for me.
I am glad you are happy once again
Two lying hearts—kept close—by never believing the truth
You were so worth the trip
But I am glad it's over …
Because I am over you.

Passionate Red

Sexual healing
Is not what I need
I need sadness to hold on
To the feeling I feed.
Make me stronger. don't walk away
Fifty years is not long enough
Forever is just a word people say
But I will hold onto eternity
Today is not just another day
Red dawn, red moon, red …

Pendulum

Ice burns
Fire cools
Fire and ice
Combine to create
Pendulum
Burning
From icy
Flames

Pirate

I am a thief.
In the night I roam
Walking away
From my happy home.

Tearing your heart
From the flag upon the pole
Stealing your dreams
My ultimate goal.

I will make you love me
Stake my claim on your soul
To my ship I steal you
Rip your body from your soul

I am the thief
Of the night; I roam
Walking away from me
To the happiness of you.

I came to steal
Your heart
Alas, you
Have stolen mine.

Pissed Off at Me

Pissed off at the world—at me.
I am upset and only I know why.
Why does he like me?
He made me mad tonight.
He laughed at me when I told him I wanted to be a teacher,
He laughed when I told him I had a foster son.
He got pissed when I told him I had a boyfriend.
Then he proceeded to tell me all these wonderful things
That he thought I needed to know about me.
He treated me like I was stupid …
What the hell? Do I have "I am an idiot, fuck me"
Written on me somewhere?
I don't trust anyone … no one at all.
I haven't been given much reason to.
I want to disappear right now,
And I don't think it's too late to.
Saying goodbye is so much easier than forever.
I just want to scream.
It doesn't really matter, because no one will ever know.
My thoughts are my prison, no room to grow.
Desert me, and turn this journal off.
Thinking out loud only gets me in trouble,
And it may not be worth the cost.

Playing Games

Player playing players games, get to hit it, tap it, but the game remains, player falls in love, player gets played

Political Upheaval

Once alone
In this dictatorship hell
I conquered
Away from freedom—wrapped
In the shackles of your emptiness.

Free at last—
For once I am—
Not within
Your brass-knuckle
Grasp.

The fly
Buzzes
Maddeningly, yet I free
Myself in his wings
Flutter

I crave what
Appeals to my
Effervescent lack
Of need for
Authoritative bullshit.

Swelling
Within my
Laden eyes
A tear begins
To escape

Satin
Embrace upon
My cheek
One tear free allows
The rest to flow

I loosen myself
From the governmental
Hold, so now
I welcome
You

To share with
You all
Who I have become
In my
Liberated world.

Perceptions

It is an amazing realization
This thing that we do
You looking at me, me looking at you.
We did an assignment in class today,
Which everyone seemed to appreciate;
I didn't like it at all.
I felt the need to deviate.
So the professor told us to write four things
We really liked about the other five people in our group.
I looked around for a moment and thought, "Good, about you?"
I felt so negative, so aggressive, so mean,
Like I was ripping them apart,
Tearing them up, warping the truth,
Perceptions scare me,
I don't know if I want to know what you see,
So I thought, and I thought, and I didn't know what else to do,
I wrote down words that did not come to my head,
Nice things I would want to hear that I could say
Then they read aloud, what it was they thought about me,
And all I could think is, "you fucking liar, that's not what you see,
Tell me the truth you bastards, tell me what you really think of me."
And then I thought for a moment.
What if that truly was what they see?
Someone nice, patient, determined, strong-willed, opinionated?
Onlookers perceptions scare me,
I don't know if I want to know what you see,
I promise I will never tell you, if you promise to never tell me.
What if the truth doesn't lie within?
What if I am not what I see?
What if I look in the mirror and I don't see
The same me you see when you look at me?
Onlookers perceptions scare me,
I don't know if I want to know what you see,
I promise I will never tell you,
If you promise to never tell me.

Positive Stimulant

No drugs
Involved
Staring
Consciously
Surviving
Eyes
Stimulating
Passion
Positive
Coolant
Take
Pressure
Wrap it
Within
Fingertips
Pull
Softly
Lust
Timely
Affection
Rubbing
Through
Heated
Thoughts
Life is
Concave …
I am not

Rainbow Love

Torn between the pages of her book and mine
Hers completely gray, mine black and white.
Loving you truly we both intend to do,
Her loving you, you loving her, me loving you.
Torn between the pages of your book and mine.
She is lost in a fantasy world of our colors intertwined.
She believes she is the only one who should consume your mind.
But colors multiply, and you do not see in black and white.
Welcome to a world of color.
Love is not blind; you can love as many colors as you want
The rainbow is made of them all.
Intertwined.

Predicament
Pre-conceived notion that I am kosher
Went to see a guy yesterday, got laid.
Weird situation, but I won't complain.
Friend came over in the morning;
I slept until afternoon, he stayed …
Can't say if he slept or not.
I woke up to some seriously heavy foreplay
It lasted for at least two hours.
It was awesome; he said, "You need some attention."
I wasn't going to argue.
He never touched my hotspots.
But he was all about me.
Baby kisses and flutterby fingers.
Seriously intense.
Intense mainly because as soon as he left,
I jumped in the shower and went to another's house.
We had a wicked fuck session. Both of us agreed.
Then I went home, took another shower,
Went with my roommate to dinner
Came home just in time for my friend to call.
Talked all night, had a good time.
We were pretty open—I was at least;
No reason to lie; I don't owe him anything.
Then he said, "I love you."
Everything from that moment on
Sucked.

Promise of a New Day
I am constantly trying to fill the
Void with people
Who truly don't matter.
Things have to change …
I can't anymore.
It will be hard, but I have had
Worse obstacles in my life, I assure you.
No more sleeping around.
I promise I am through.
I will not do it any longer,
Not for me, not for you.
I want to be healthy,
I want to be loved.
I want to be held by hands
That give more than a fuck.
I am in the mood for a relationship.
I quit all the nonsensical bullshit.

Ready to Live

Stuck in a hole
    I dug for myself …
        Don't lend me a hand
            I don't want out …
                But don't throw the dirt over my head just yet
                    I am just taking a rest …

Provider

Please don't let me hear you call him stupid once again
You tell him he makes bad decisions
You keep him down to build you up
Do you know what you are doing to him?

You treat him like one of your children
You make him feel unworthy
You make his mistakes public so that he is flogged by all
Do you know what you are doing to him?

You have made mistakes too—do you bring those up in public?
You have made bad decisions too—do you realize this?
You kicked him out, changed the locks—then ask him back
Do you know what you are doing to him?

You are the only person he's ever fought to keep
You are the one he thinks of—constantly
You gave him three beautiful children—then left
Do you know what you are doing to him?

You are making him love to hate to love you
You are making him a scared little boy
You are making him pull away from everyone
You have all the control.

Push Me, Pull You

I know you love the way you feel
When you are with me—
The strength is real.
But I also know just what to do
To make you happy—within you.
I'm not what you want, not what you need
So in love with the emotional fuck,
Just can't say that I see what you see.
We are both hot at the moment
Pulling each other close
But what of when I'm hot and
You are cold—push me, pull you.
You told me to leave, and I did;
You called me to come back, and I did, gladly.
I was cold, and you were hot.
I asked you to leave but you would not.
Baby, these feelings will always be real.
I will be forever, no matter how you feel.
The fear I have that is real within you—
What if the frozen heart came through?
Your heart ice—pushing me away,
My heart, fire, refusing to stay.
That will be the ultimate defeat.
The true ending of our love.
I want to always know how you feel,
Not so I can hurt you, but so that I won't.
The way you feel is what keeps us together;
I will keep pushing, if you will keep pulling.

Run

Loser
Flower
Wrapped in sin
Blackened—
Dancing chaotic emotion
From the pain within—
Run

Repercussion

Entangled in the moment
Squashed by meager defeat
The pain from this feeling
The willingness to release
Drama, waiting on the other hand
Holy ghosts—on devil's land
Torridly spinning, unequivocal stand
I have nothing to prove

Rain

Rain pouring outside my window
Calling out to you into the night.
Knowing you sleep alone,
Knowing I am alone inside.

I fight to clear my thoughts of you,
But plagued I feel I must be;
With every touch of my own skin,
I long for you to set me free.

Sadness envelops the darkness,
Redness grasps my gentle face,
Tears begin to fall in vain,
I scream for you in the night.

Like two dragons fleeing,
I hope to someday be
Alone with you in our dreams.
A mystical cave. You holding me

A place for us to hide,
To make love, to be as one
As I lie here in the silence of my room,
Dying in your arms

I fight,
For you to know precisely
How much you mean to me.
Rain-the tears I cry.

Representation
She borrowed a quarter from her lover
Promised to give it back
The quarter, representation of nothing
Broken in half at her welding table
She returned it to him
With the knowledge that this quarter,
Now a worthless keepsake,
Had become a representation of her
Leaving
Now everything is a darker shade of gray.

Respect
Respect your children …
If you give them a chore chart,
Make sure your name is on it …
And follow through.

Restlessly Wanting You
I know you're scared.
Fuck it, I'm scared too.
But I want to give it a try.
It doesn't matter why.
Last night for the first time
In so long I can't remember
I felt like needing you.
In my bed alone, you and me.
But I didn't prove to be what you wanted,
What you thought you'd need.
I don't care if it proves to be a waste of time.
Don't want to be your girl
Not your band of gold to show your friends
Just your lover.
Damn woman, I've got me so twisted for you.
Sunrise and I am thinking about you.
Somewhere you sleep, subconsciously
Thinking about me.
How do I know?
Power of persuasion planted
By an intelligent mind—
Mine.

Return the Favor

No one will ever be able to return the favor.
I'll never get mine.
Maybe that's how it is supposed to be—
We'll have to see.
Yeah, I'll let them come over—and sit—
And watch my world revolve around them—
No I won't expect the same from them—
Trust me, I know better. Yeah, they can call my phone
But I know better than to ever call them
Yes, I've done this before—
Yes, I know you'll leave me for her, and
Yeah, I'll try to stay a friend to you.
But I know too well, six months from now you will be
Nonexistent. No one will ever understand.
They can never love you as I do,
So unconditional, so true.
But it's ok—walk away.
I'll never try to stop you.
Or expect you to return the favor.

Retreat

Into myself where I belong
I wonder if ever for me you'll long

Being aware I cannot see
How you could want someone like me

I will walk away, I will retreat
Love can be its own defeat

So many years old, just too young to see
What you could do for someone like me

I am aware of what you may feel
But I cannot strive to keep it real

What would your friends do?
What will I expect from you?

I am overly assertive, true
But I do not want to hurt you.

I know my place, where I should be
Less worry for you—I will retreat back to me.

Saturated

Blood covers my body, and I am drenched in your spirit—
Soiled by your love, covered from head to toe
In an image of your feelings.
I am worthless—drowning in all of you—
Saturated by the emotionless keep—
And all I can do is love you.
For you know not what you do to me,
With your blanket of blood-covered love

Scared

Scared of the
Tears
That bring the
Rain
Fear of the
Love
That brings the
Pain

Rocket Science of Self-Degradation

Manipulation, lying.
It is not rocket science.
I am good at this game of screw them and leave;
I know it is not healthy,
I know they all want more,
But I know deep within me
I am better off alone.
If I sleep with them,
I get what I want,
Pretend to like them,
Sweet-talk the hell out of them,
Maybe even call them a few times
To mess with their minds;
Then walk away, out of the blue.
It's just so damn easy to get
What I want that way.
I stay single, live life my way,
Don't have to prove anything to anyone
Do what I want to.
Morally aware of the scars I could cause.
Never cheated, never had to …
Great sex whenever I wanted it,
Spectacular …
He was so busy doing what he wanted that
He never got in my way!
But now, I run around like a dog in heat
Constantly looking for the next sex treat.
This will eventually destroy my life …
But I will survive.
Here's to great sex,
No kids,
No lies,
No foundations.
No problems manipulating me …
I am so damn good at that.

Scream

Rancid blood
Drifted dream
Run into the fog
Listen to the scream
Fight for the vision
Of you within me
Stimulate my mind,
Make me scream.

Sanctuary

Sacrificed by the tree, I am the fallen leaf.
Able to blow in the wind, left, forgotten.
Reassurance from the rain, reconnected to the ground,
Given sanctuary in the cluster of detritus.
You and I are such similar creatures.
I am the leaf, and you are the tree.
You have let me go, and so I wander
From the mountains I come down
Flowing free among the clouds.
Blowing in the wind,
Intertwine in the rain, falling to the ground,
Where we will someday meet again.

Satisfaction

Satisfy the demon, from the love within my happiness you linger,
Only to satisfy your demon. I don't want to fuck you.
The feeling we shared, I flipped the switch,
I'm sick of you trying, sick of your shit.
Create awareness, for you to play
For me, I need to walk away.
Satisfy the angel within …

Safe Environment

I'm not interested in hurting you
And I don't expect anything
But you got me twisted for you
In a way I haven't been …

I enjoy the way I feel—and don't—
It's not about the chase
I'm intrigued by this friendship
I promise not to take advantage of us.

I don't know what you want from me—
I want to give you myself.
You know there are others
But I want to work on this with you.

Maybe I feel challenged,
Maybe I know it will never work,
Maybe I feel like you could love me ,
Maybe I just know it's temporary and I am intrigued—

But damn, I want to give it a try.
What are you thinking? Are you free?
Are you scared of what everyone else will think?
This is a safe environment for you

You are in control
You can stay or you can go
I want you to be happy
With or without me.

Sex You Up

The look, enough to excite me.
To feel the warmth you create
Within me, within my soul.
Touch me, taste me,
Like only you can.
In the way of emotion
With your experienced hand.
You—only you—
Know how to please me
The way I want you to—
Because you know
My emotions need to be touched
With your passion.
Look at me, damn you—
Don't try to hide these feelings.
Pay attention to your vile mind,
You might like what it reveals.
Slip your fingers down
Impatient as you are—
I want to hold your impurities
Within my creative heart.
Let me see
All of the wetness I create
Set your pheromones free.
Nibble on my ankles,
Rub my nose behind your knee,
Set your hand upon my head,
Reposition me.
Take control, let me be a part
Of the wetness I create
I'm in the mood to eat.
Wrap my lips around your spot,
Dip my tongue within
Taste your salt, your candy
Moan some more as I slip my fingers in—
Let me take complete control—
Do you have the strength to come again?
I wasn't finished tasting you—
It's where I want to be—
Ravish you—with all of me,
I'm ready.

Teacher

She sits in class and writes down what she thinks.
Everything beautiful. Everything surreal.
The day passes by so slowly, yet so unequivocally.
Complacent in her duress, she waits, subconsciously withering.
The day is cold, dreary and dry. The time slowly passes by.
Paper is rustling, air keeps kicking on,
Daylight inexplicably come and gone.
1:20 in the afternoon. Already beat. caffeine calling, but should not drink.
Drained by this day and its nonsensical nature.
Longing to be where she is—wishing this was my class.
Dancing around the room
Making a scene, teaching knowledge
Creating memories.

Shoes

At twenty-five, I have married and divorced.
It's been four years since I have
Been in a steady relationship. My friends tell me I am
Afraid to commit, then they call me a player because I
Date so many different people. You know, I keep telling
Them, I had a pair of shoes that I bought in 1999. They
Lasted two years and they were extremely comfortable.
Those shoes decided they needed to walk a different path.
Now, when I look for a pair of shoes to purchase, I try
Them on, keep them on for a little while, and put them
Back if I decide they won't do. Analogies aside, there is no law
That says we have to be married, and
For those of you who run for the
Whole commitment aspect of life,
I hope you find a great pair of running shoes.
For the rest of us, heels and
Slippers will do just fine.
Not meant for walking in, just
For looking great or feeling great
For a little while.

Sitting

Sitting at the table
Working at life
Watching you walk on by.
The look in your eyes says you want me—
And I am ok with that.
The thought of your tongue on my lips,
Your flesh upon my soul—
I'm trying to cry out.
Yearning for more.
I don't care what they say.
This is for me—for you …
Someday.

Sleeping With You

I have been sleeping with you for weeks … Seems like
So much longer. At times you really upset me,
Other times are great … Go figure. Not your girl,
Don't care to be. In the moment, I am happy
Being single and having fun, and I hope you are too.
Don't worry, I don't expect anything from you.
The hickey on your neck last night, the funniest thing,
You know you don't have to lie to me …
A birthmark that you cover with make-up every day? Classic!
I so don't care … No really,
I am not a jealous person, and of course I laughed
And of course you told me the truth, and of
Course you realized that I really don't care because I
Really don't care about you … Not as anything more than a
Friend … It will be fine. You will see. I enjoy spending
Time with you, but as a friend; that is all I
Want you to be …

Stealing Virginity

Commercial penetration of
America's kids.
Branding the children and
Trying to get there first.

Soft Pink Dress

Soft pink caresses your skin as you walk.
It flows over you like silk in the wind,
The ripples of your flow attract me, bring me in—
Push my motivations from another—
Touch me—turn me—longing, yearning ...
Pouring through me like fresh melted chocolate,
So sweet, so rich, so free.
Thicken baby, thicken for me, all over you,
All over me. This is where I want to be ...
In place of your soft pink dress.

Someday I'll Be Good Enough

You made me forget
My fears when you wanted to
You knew just what to do to
Make them subside
You kissed away my anger,
The demons we tried to hide.

I knew this time I had found
Someone to build my life with
It was inevitable.
You are not perfect
But you are perfect
For me.

You are a wonderful lover
And an amazing friend
After all my life has put me through
I knew you were safe,
It was ok to be with you
What we had will never end …

When you feel sad and lonely,
You'll think of me
I filled that void so easily.
When you feel like you're not good enough,
Remember our conversations,
And how I made you feel.

Remember our first kiss,
Sitting on the couch,
The look in my eyes,
The smell of my skin,
This feeling so powerful,
It will never end.

One day you will realize,
This love was truly real …
Until then, I guess you'll never know,
How much I was willing to love you …
You're gone now. I guess
I wasn't good enough … again.

Struggling

I am fucking struggling once again.
Try so hard to help everyone
Lost in their semi-catastrophe
My yellow rose is drowning
I fear I watered it too much
Suffocated it with my love
Showered it with too much emotion.
I believe it is ok—my yellow rose—
If you feel the need to wilt—
Breathe death's freedom …

Scarlett

Someone once told me,
"You are a beautiful flower; bloom on."
I am afraid I did,
And now almost all of my petals are gone.

Wilted, down to my last petal
Crying for the rain
Screaming for just one drop of moisture
To drown this treacherous pain.

I am sorry that I looked to you
To be a single drop
I was hoping you would quench my thirst.
But it is obvious that you will not.

Simply passing away
The sun is beating down
Looking for a single tear
Realizing in the distance—a cloud.

Hope for new life, a cloud to hide the sun
Even though you could not be the rain
You were still a seraph—
A friend you have become.

Vines alive,
I've latched onto the walls,
Alive again,
I have begun to crawl.

I can walk away if you want me to,
Just give me a little time,
But I would like to stick around,
If the decision is to be mine.

Spitfire

I am a ball of raging fire
Red, yellow, orange, and black,
Burning wild, roaring free.
You are ice thrown onto my fire.

But you alone cannot tame me.
I am the demon within the girl
Whom you complement so well
But your piece of ice is weak,

And I am this angel's hell.
To rid her of her demon,
You must bring a group of friends,
She can withstand your desire.

She can burn you where you stand.
One ice cube is not enough
You will need many,
Many more.

Sometimes

Sometimes we feel what we hear—
And that distorts the truth behind the words.

Sweat

She sips the sweat From the pores of his affection Unclear, yet so pure
Holding tightly to the bottle Empty—with his love She sips the sweat
From the memory Of his kiss Tired Alone in the moment
Reminiscing Lying in bed Tears drip From her eyes
As they fall Uncontrollable Tears—sweat like rain In the night
She calls to him He awakens She turns to him In the silence
Of the darkness Within the room They embrace She sips the sweat
From his body Tender love made She sits up In a cold mess
From the bottle—vodka Mistaken for her lover's Sweat

Snow Come Down

You sit in the window—looking out over the snow-covered ground,
The moonlight reflecting off the glistening crystals. You feel yourself
Dreaming of being a part of it all. You run your fingers
Through your hair, resting your elbow on your windowsill. Then you go—

No further hesitation—running through the dark house to the door.
Your face in the wind, uninhibited, racing into the icy night.
Body engulfed by the powdery presence kicked into the air
By your feet's flutter. Cold and numb, your body becomes
From the wicked wind as it whips your naked flesh. The blueness
Of the moon's reflected light in the air, the beauty that surrounds you—
You fall into the uninviting snow. Engulfed in the wetness,
You freeze—instantly—holding tightly to the burning pain.
It is beginning to snow again.

More pain, more beauty; smile and laugh as you stare into the wind.
Wrap your hand around the freezing doorknob, give it a twist, a shove.
Feel the rush of the heat. Stand at the window
And reminisce as the falling snow covers your footprints.
Wonder what was more enjoyable: watching the beauty from your window,

Or becoming a part of it—no matter how much it hurt.
You walk to the fireplace, sit to thaw. Knowing inside
It's worth risking it all. Look at the door and for a moment contemplate
Going again—running into the snowfall. Hear her voice from the bedroom,
Ripping you from your thoughts, calling to you: "Baby, come to bed."
You stand and sigh—turning away from the fire you walk toward her.

Look back at the front door—once more—then open the door to her room.

Take Notice

The times when I am
Most happy …
I do not write
so many months gone for
False hopes and lost loves

Team

Trying to keep up with the boys,
I lose all of me fighting for you
You are in need of satisfaction
That I cannot give to you
What you want, and what I give
Will never complete the need in you.
Why does it have to be this way?
Why is it all about you?

Subordinating Conjunctions Free My Mind

Although you've seen me smile
Since I walked away
Because you never asked me
So that I'd never say
I walked away without telling you.

As you sat in your room listening to my voice on the line
Whether or not I am crying runs rampant through your mind
Because you thought I loved you--and yet it was so easy for me to say goodbye
Although you never asked me and so I never told you why
My emotions stay stained within me and you will never see me cry.

Unless the morning light shines a shadow of you on my wall
After the restless sleep I forsake
As long as you are in my presence
While I lie here and dream of you in my arms when I am awake
You will not know how you saturated my heart before I walked away.

Tainted You

Truth is: I am scared.
Truth is: I cannot do anything about it.

Fact is: don't worry, it's not your battle.
Fact is: My battle has not yet begun, and yet it is over.

Tainted
There are so many things I feel.
I am just an ordinary girl
Though everyone thinks me so extraordinary
I just don't think I'll ever understand

What makes me so intriguing?
What makes me so beautiful?
Why not her?
It's the thrill of the chase you love so much, not me …

I am a challenge to you and you love every minute of it.
What am I supposed to do now? Walk away?
Suck it up? Well fuck,
I guess I am screwed.

You all want to love me,
You take the challenge on,
Then you figure out what I'm about,
And you pack your shit and leave.

Well, I'll save you the trouble,
Lay down for you
Fuck me quickly, so I can move on
Get over the likes of you.

I am not in the mood for foolish games.
Been to hell and back
Not right love—it's not for me
I am through with you …

Tears

Tears of melancholy rain
Not right love
Is not rightly wrong
Baby I do love you
But I have
To move on.
Tears of disarray
Make me strong

Treacherous

The friend
I have in you
I no longer need
    I walk
    Away
    Satisfied
With this realization
That I am
Worth more love
    Than your
    Bleeding heart
    Could ever show.

The Bird

Laughing, I twist,
Free, alone, satisfied,
I am
The bird, being carried away,
To a place, a place I love.

Tumultuous Oleander

Grow wild in my orchard,
So that I may feed off
Your sweet flavorful juices.

Two Lying Hearts

You are no different than the rest
And yet, I long to hear your voice
To see you smile, to feel you naked, close to me.

You lied, you stole, you cheated, you disguised
The mask you wear in your everyday life will leave
A vulnerable impression upon everyone you face.

You tried to use my words against me.
You said you wanted to leave; I told you to;
When you left, you said it was my doing.

What a wicked game you play.
I guess you are just sharing your weakness in that way.
I am not for you— you are not for me.

You and she make a wonderful couple …
I am glad you have gone back home
Two lying hearts, never believing the truth.

You were so worth the trip
But I am glad it's over …
Because I am over it.

The Last Day

Today is the last day of the year
Tomorrow I will wake up closer
To the life I need to live
To the love I have to feed
I am in control of nothing
You are in control of me
Today is the last day of the year
Next year—are you ready for me?

The Most Beautiful Part of the Rose

The most beautiful part of the rose? Its root.
Without a root, there would be no stem to hold the thorns
No thorns to protect the petals from envious girls' desires
No leaves to collect the nutrients to feed the beauty that we see
No beauty to create such a profitable market on holidays
Yes, without the rose's root
There would be no rose at all

The Phantom Lover

Emerald satin covers her naked body,
Crimson embers from the fire
Create primitive undress
Ghostly whispers
From the breeze that seeps through the unopened window
She calls to him in her sleep
On the seas, below the hollow moon,
The sailor screams her name
Longing to be within her
To satisfy the primal lust
Two souls reach out to one another Caught up in passion's dance
She is shattered in a moment where she thinks she feels his touch,
The fire cavorts, casting shadows of heated flesh.
She runs her fingers across her nakedness,
Down her neck, across her breast, to her enchanted spider webs.
Her fingers dance within her, as she calls out his name.
Across the winds, through the night, passion sparks his flame.
Yearning for her, through the night he begins to caress,
Her thoughts, her body, through his nakedness.
Slipping into sleep, satisfied, complete,
Cries of joy split the night as fulfillment reaches its peak
She calls out his name. Their souls become one.
Crying out into the heat of prudent honesty,
She is awakened by the release of the phantom's erotic caress
Clutching her empty bed, tangled in her sheets,
Pillow between her legs, soaking up the dampness
Sleep puts out the fire, as they finish their lovemaking quest.

The Rose Bud

Solitary confinement brings me to my knees,
The petals of the red rose in the winter do freeze
But as the summer comes around, and new birth recreates,
I become the enchanted one, and loneliness dies in its place

The Romantics

I had a young man come into my store last night.
He gave me a copy of Vivaldi
A gift he'd been meaning to give me
He couldn't wait to see me listening to it
And then he left. Romantic?
Yes. The idea of it sure made me melt.
So original, so unexpected, so not chocolate and roses
I have no idea who this kid was; I've only seen him in my store;
He comes in all the time—but he won't come in anymore.
I don't think I gave him the reaction he was looking for.
Damn, and I actually thought that was pretty impressive.
I listened to Vivaldi the rest of the night,
And I enjoyed every minute of it.
My heart sinks …
Will I ever be good enough?

The Unfeeling Kiss

Surprised by the emotion in the kiss we shared
Used to kissing and not feeling impaired
Sat back and contemplated never kissing you again.
Not sure I wanted to feel; not sure I wanted it to end.
What do you need, what do you want from me?
I feel like I am about to give it all away.
But I am not sure if that is going to keep me free.
So far-so good; I have been real, no reason to lie.
I feel you have been dishonest—but that is okay.
Soon you will see I don't lie to you—and you don't have to lie to me.
The power in this kiss made me weak.
Don't know what to make of it, what to think.
Simply taking it one day at a time
Impatient—yes you are, but tomorrow will wait,
If these feelings are true
No need to rush I will allow the intensity, won't dismiss
Intrigued by the potency of a kiss
Aware of how you are feeling; unsure if I care.
At the moment, all I know is that I am going to get hurt
And I am loving every second anyway.
Been hurt before. I know my worth;
Not in the mood to indulge in an unfeeling kiss
Wanting to enjoy these feelings at least for the moment.
Hoping you understand the game in our control:
Both of us masters, both of us whores.
Indulge me with your mastery. Loving the flavors of your kisses,
I will sacrifice my freedom—for the moment …

The Second Chance

In the river, there is a sound, a hum
From the creatures beneath the water's inky surface.
It sends shivers down my spine.
Guilt has never hit me before, as it is hitting me right now.
The night is dark. The river is screaming to me.
Night after night the wind whispers back
The memories of that ghastly evening.
I was fifteen years old, a sophomore in high school.
I had been drinking with friends at a party
Just around the corner from the local skating rink.
I never meant to hurt her; I only wanted to kiss her.
I never meant for it to go as far as it did.
She should have never said no.
Then it would have been all right.
We could have finished what we started and I would never have
Had to hurt her.
I enter the darkness of my room where paranoia sets in.
The hairs on my skin begin crawling like leeches.
The room is spinning. I have to get out of this house.
To the front door I run; the coldness clasps my face
With a bitter sting, like a knife cutting away at my flesh.
Heading for the forest, the darkness stuns my sanity.
For miles I see nothing but the reflection of the moon
Following me. I run as fast as my legs will carry me.
Guilt fills my already rapidly beating heart,
And the wind chases me like a phantom.
My body tumbles uncontrollably down the hill.
A thousand thoughts race through my mind
As I reach for passing tree branches.
All I can think is, "I am sorry." It's not supposed
To be this way. I yell into the darkness, "I am sorry!"
I splash into the water, grabbing for anything to stay afloat;
There is nothing, nothing to grab!
So cold. I feel a sharp sting over my right eye,
Warm blood flows heavily down my face.
A passing branch—grabbing, hauling
Lifting myself onto the bank of the river
Then collapse.
In the clear crisp moonlight I awake.
On the riverbank, cold and alone, I lie on the
Dew-soaked grass. Dazed and a little confused,
Looking up at the sky, I make the decision to return to my past,
Which for so long I have regretted, and
Finally make amends with myself.

The Rope
One end around my neck
And one around his

If I pull too hard
He will die

If he pulls too hard
I will die

A pain in the neck
Long, winding, thick, rough

Wrapped around
Our necks—tightly

Stealing breath
From us both—equally

Pulling us in two
Different directions

Not allowing us
To walk together

Not permitting us
To stand—stable

Me pulling—you pulling
One of us will die

Your end fraying
Mine becoming stronger

I am dying
Trying to hold on to life

Drowning in the raw pain
You begin to cry

The rope has won
And you—its prize …

The Touch, the Taste

Sitting across the table from you
Wanting, waiting.
Listening to you speak
Your words, your voice—everything
Making me wet.
Feeling confident
Not in my physical presence
But definitely in my sexuality
I begin my groove
Move to the couch
I rub your neck with my fingertips
Your back—slowly, softly,
To your stomach; sensual touch
Letting you know I want to fuck.
Impatiently I slip my hands into your pants
Grasping your solid manhood.
Looking to you for a reaction
Carefully I caress your stomach with my tongue.
The simple sounds you make keep me wet.
Placing my mouth around your cock
I wet the head of the shaft with my throat
Your moaning makes me impatient to taste you
Slowly, deeply, wetly I suck
Following your movement
Faster, harder, deeper.
My patience wears thin
Your hands slip down my pants to my clit
Rubbing slowly. Quickly
I remove my clothing
You begin to suck my breasts, my neck
I return the favor
On your neck
In your ear

Skimming all over your body
With just my fingertips.
Your smell makes me hot
I can't wait any longer
Climb on top
Pause long enough for you to slip a condom on
Bend over the kitchen counter
Slip you in from behind.
The initial penetration makes us simultaneously gasp
Throbbing, thumping my ass against your pelvis
Gyrating my hips,
Harder, faster I move
You against me, me enveloping you
To our rhythm we rock
To poetry we serenade
The moment in a song of your breath with mine
My body slapping against yours
Your sweat making my skin's song rhyme.
Rocking in time
Your cock in my pussy
You rub my back with your fingertips
I raise my hips to your invasion
You pull me to you
Ready for release
Harder you shove
Harder, faster, then—explode
Smile on your face
Time spent with you
Was worth the chase
This kitty caught the mouse
And her pussy loved the taste
We'll have to rhyme again sometime
Won't let this go to waste.

Walk Away

The fire burns within me
My life is anger to be defined
I walk quietly into the woods
To hide my tears, to have them seen
No, I'd rather die
Snow envelops my fire
Dancing upon the embers
Coldness clasps my insides
Burning more than fire ever could
The desire within the fire—burns
Leaves the ice—the fear that I am not
Good enough—engulfs
Does not enchant me anymore
Walking through the dark, deep woods
Snow melting out of spite
Creates the embers within my soul—burning
My charbroiled heart smolders once more
I know you do not love me—
Sputtering fire—melting snow
You love only the idea of me—
Burning fire, falling snow—glistening
Together we burn
It does not mean our love cannot be
I walk slowly back inside
To where the embers await me
Burn together—I'd much rather do
Fire and ice will emerge
As one single entity.
Symbolism is a friend.

Honey

There is so much that I can't do
But there is so much that I can
Won't you let me free you of your pain?
Sit with me, talk with me, allow yourself to be free.
Taste the flavor of optimism.
Relax; you are growing up way too fast.
You are nine, not thirteen; why so sour?
Do you feel like you have something to prove?
Do you not care what you are doing to me—
Or maybe this is why you are doing it—
Do you think it is all about me?
All about your brother?
Do you see how much this is about a missing "us"
Because you do not allow it to be.

Anxious

This overwhelming feeling of anxiety that
Chokes my indifference
Leaves me numb to your frozen smile.
The lack of ambition in your stance.
My beautiful child, you feel what I fear.
I know what you are going through—
I know that is not what you want to hear.
I've been where you are—
Hell, I struggle with it every day.
You are my reason for living—
And I cherish you so much for loving me your way.
The fear of not being good enough consumes me every day.
Baby girl, I wish you could see past this
Blindfold on your heart—
Your sadness is tearing us apart.
Without you, I would be lost?
Baby girl, I love you— I need you—can't that be enough?
I wish you could see all the good there is in the world—
I promise to help you any way that I can—
All you have to do is let me love you—
Be here for you—
Struggle with you—
Baby girl, it's all I can do …
Please take my hand and let me
Fight this battle with you.

Baby Girl

Sweet girl, so innocent.
Bottles up the madness within
In her own home.
"And who really cares?" she says.
"Nobody will, when the ones that gave me life deny me so."
And we scream to her, "what do you mean nobody cares?"
"And if that's the way you feel, why am I even here?"
She runs to her room—instead of talking—
We know what she's going through—
What we don't know is why—
and every time we try to talk all we end up with is a fight.
She gives us nothing—no reason for the fuel in her fire—
Holding onto nothing but anger and sadness
My frivolous attempts are creating nothing but madness
She's ready—throw up her hands and give it all up.
For God's sake—
She's nine years old!!
Somebody help me—
I just need to know what she is going through
Why can't I take her pain?
Please somebody my hands aren't large enough to hold it all
And there's so much more left within—
I'm on my knees now—
Praying to whoever will listen—
I need her to be happy—
Somebody just show me the way ...

Thirsty?

You must drink the Kool-Aid in order to understand
How the question plus the answer equals
Being completely satisfied.

The best answer to give a child when you don't know the answer
Could quite simply be, "I don't know."
But should you leave it at that?

Or do you try to find the answer
Together?
I choose the second option.

To Me, From Me

Alone, under satin sheets of blue
In the still of my room I lie naked.
Silence surrounds my beating heart;
I feel you. In the presence of nothingness,
I smell your breath, so sweet, so pure.
The curtains from the window dance wildly;
A distraction, to keep my mind from you.
My blue-eyed abandonment, how I wish you were here
The mirror gives me nothing but pity and fear.
My better half, where have you gone?
I sit here confused, scared, and alone.
Where have you gone?

To Feel

To feel life through your emotions
I wonder what my life would be
Holding tightly—never letting go
I wonder—would you see me?
If I became you for one single day
Would we be friends anymore?
It is just so hard to say.
I'm not sure that you could handle being me—
Not even for one day.
My emotions are solid, varied.
I know myself very well.
For you to be me might scare you.
To the point that you might tell me to
Go to hell.
It is just too hard to tell.
I challenge you to see you
Through my eyes, my emotions
Can you take the time to be you
With all of me?
What I really need to know is
Not if you can
But are you willing?
It is just too hard to understand.
I want you … I do
But I want you to want me—to want you too.
No more games.
I will be with you—through you—
And not through me.
It is just so hard to be me.

To Let Go

Today I am in awe of a person
I enjoy spending time with, I enjoy talking to, I enjoy touching,
If for no other reason than to give her a hug.
She and I are connected in a way I do not understand.
She and I could stay the best of
friends but is that all I am cut out to be?
Friends forever? When will I be able to take these wonderful
Connections and make them more? I placate her, I tell her
I am not the relationship type; I make a great friend,
But other than that, I am not good enough.
She has to believe me—not the part of not being good enough, but
I have been single for over a year. And before that
I was married but separated for 3 years.
So none of my friends has ever seen me in a relationship.
This makes it very easy for people to believe me when I say
I am great at being alone. But, I
have to say … I want a chance to prove
Myself wrong. Will it happen? I guess we'll have to see,
Won't we? Until tomorrow … I wait for the opportunity, to be good enough …
For one.

Today

Today is the day I find out what will change in me.
I will forever be a loser, or I will emerge gracefully.
I am graduating in three days.
But I have an exam today at noon
That may just be the death of me.
I have such a hard time with this General Ecology
Bullshit. I studied for a month with two different tutors.
We will see today if it pays off,
Or if I am taking summer classes!
Well, my mind is on so many other things,
I can't even concentrate on this damn exam.
I am in the middle of moving right now.
Packing, taking a four-hour round trip
Every day, sometimes twice a day.
I am so tired, and on top of that I have an
Upper respiratory infection,
So my mind is foggy with medications,
My head hurts from all this thinking,
I start a new job in two weeks,
I am going on vacation next week,
I am going temporarily insane.
It is so hard to breathe.

Too Damn Good

People do not try to understand
How fucking easy it is for me to close down my heart and
Walk away—too easy.
I am wondering if anyone will ever care to understand me.
Probably not because I am too busy psychoanalyzing, scaring them.
People are incredible. I sweep them off their feet, scare them to tears,
Make them fall fast in love' then they become consumed by "Is this too good to be true?"
"Could this be real?" "Can she be lying?" "How did she sweep me off my feet?"
Walk away—I never wanted you to stay. You'll never understand.

Tortured

Walking
Sipping my indifference
Through your straw
I trip—
On your drink
I swallowed
Nothing
And yet,
I feel so—
    Much a part of you
    I am drowning
    In your poignant loneliness
You are an emotional
Wake-up call
In the cold
Drink of your morning
Rapture
Saddened
By the image
Of you
On my mind—knowing
    I sipped to my death
    The blood of your stone cold
    Non-beating heart

Too Into You

I've been around,
I'm in the business,
And oh, you are fucked
Your world is finished.
Loving you, loving me
Can't you tell, can't you see?
I'm the one, I'll fuck your world …
Let me be your little girl
Hold me close within your arms …
Phantom love, meant for you …
I'll never walk away—you'll see
I'm too into you.

Totally Dreaming

I fell asleep last night. I knew I wasn't supposed to,
But it doesn't matter.
I had the most awesome dream
About a baby.
I am not sure if I had it, or if someone else did.
But I felt so safe, standing around, holding it.
Looking into this baby's eyes relaxed me—
So amazing.
He was in my dream.
He was walking around with me,
I don't know what to think.
Another was in the dream too.
Telling me he always knew in God's time it would happen.
Well, like I said before,
I do not know whose baby it was,
And I am not going to assume,
But it doesn't truly matter,
Because the emotions of
Holding that baby within my arms
Were more than I can express.
I hope I have more dreams like that one.
It's dreams like that
That encourage me to sleep!

Tokin'

Took it upon myself to take control
No longer your lover, no longer your whore.
Bent you over, took you in
Emotionally captured you
While you were least expecting
Took you out, had a laugh, passed you
Around, took you back
Held you within my head
Fucked you from my core
Out where we could be seen
In the end it was meant to be
Me fucking loving you
You fucking me
You held me in your bed
Made love from your core
But out where we could be seen
I was treated like a whore
Once more.

Wanting You

Wanting you—oh, but certainly not needing you.
I sit here thinking about you, constantly.
I can't wait for these feelings to disappear.
I wish you knew the truth, but you never will.
You neither want nor need to know.
I don't understand how you can let her
Do what she does to you.
I am in awe of the things you take from her,
Of the things I am capable of doing to you.
Yes, I have treated men the way she treats you—
Like shit.
But you were different. I never wanted to treat you that way.
You will never understand.
Our love is so amazingly thick. You stay with her out of fear
Because she is a comfort for you. But I was love—and that just
Was not good enough—was it?
What can I do? I vow to try harder
To be a good person, to be free, to be happy to try my hardest
To do good—for once in my life. What do I do now?
Walk away from yesterday and toward tomorrow.
Damn, I need to learn to say no.
My life would be a lot easier that way.
Well, I have always had that problem—
Haven't I?

Wasted

Wasted time spent on you
Walking always sideways
Nothing left or to do
You don't want me to go
And yet you say you do?
Man, get over yourself
Your life with me
Will be a lot easier that way.
I don't care if you disagree
Get over yourself
And start getting to know me
You'll see
We'll both start walking upwards if
And when you do.

Was I Dreaming

When I felt you touch me?
I loved the way you talked
To me last night
You are amazing.
Can I keep you?
Will you be with me
Until our hearts give way
To the incapability of loving
And enjoying it?
We talk so well
Communicate effectively
I apologize for my need
To nitpick about absolutely nothing
I swear it doesn't matter when
You leave things out; I do it too
I swear it doesn't mean anything
When I laugh, smile, pick on you,
Dream of you, talk erratically.
It all shows my love for you.
I was dreaming
This cannot be real.
Or can it?

Wonderful

What we have is so wonderful
So assured and so all alone
What would they do if we walked away?
From all of them, and started
Our own world.
I would hold you in my arms
Until we fell

When All Else Fails

When all else fails
And the world seems screwed up
You hold out your hand
But don't give up
The fight that is not yours
Is not worth the struggle
Hold out your heart
But don't break for the trouble
When all else fails
And you see you can't go on …
Call me for a helping hand
Together we will move on.

Drowning

When the fury of my tears
Creates a river of denial
I know it's time to start drowning

Willing

Where did my life go?
Hello, life, where are you?
I am saddened by the thought
That my life has deserted me.
To struggle through death, forever …
Is this really what hell feels like?
Or have I just lost my way?
I reach out from my soul to grab
The next creature willing
To hold onto me …

Wings

Time and time again we change the world
On **the wings of a butterfly**
We **soar; we open our mouths and reveal words with no floor**
They **flutter around, buzzing ignorant ears**
By **and by we change the world**
Forever

Who I Am

I am who I am
And without you I am
Who I am
And who I am
I love

Wild Winds

Wild winds blow torridly
The sky screams out in vain.

The laughter rings in from the heavens
Hell's angels let their wings stretch.

Wild winds from wings do grow
Hell and heaven—no one knows.

Fighting all to rule and grow
Wild wings from winds do flow.

Fighting beating wings arise
Heaven's angels fight to fly.

The rain beats down,
The heavens sting.

The floors of heaven
Start to scream.

Hell's angels have begun to slow,
Heaven's angels grasp triumph.

Wild winds cease to blow
Heaven has won the sun will show.

Surrendered hate, forbidden love.
Fight won solemnly, heavens above.

Within the Pit of Your Heart

Deep down you'll find me
Drowning in everyone else's tears.
Finding satisfaction in the ripe odor of soil and
Rain which envelopes my being.
Controlled—holding on—falling
Hands to my side, backward
Into the rain-soaked loam.
Splashing the mud—above me, around me.
I swallow the filth that encapsulates my soul—
And I wake suddenly—
Choked to death by your arms wrapped
Lovingly around my suffocated emotions.
Kiss away your salty sadness and receive a smile.
Ripped to shards of nothing—left to feel beautiful for spite.
You holding me tighter, holding me tonight.

Where Now

Where the fuck is the love
That you say you feel
That you say you share
That you say you want,
That you say you need?
You can't give love,
Without first loving yourself.
Don't tell me you love me,
Kind soul
Tell me you are weak,
Tell me you are scared,
Tell me you are trying—
These are words I will believe.
But do not tell me you love me.
I am sick of your lies.

Wishful Thinking

I wish that you would stop all the nonsense
Stop all the bullshit

I wish my life could take a steady stop
Not go anywhere. Not make me hot

I am tired of the temperamental bullshit
Walk away baby …

Time on—Time off
In need of the feeling you offer …

Alone, I am satisfied
Not afraid to love—or to leave.

My day is valuable
Why can't you see?

I can't love you—
'Cause you don't love me.

Withered

Into a hole I crawl, to hide.
No one will ever understand how much
I want to feel – but don't.
People who say they can read me
Make me laugh inside, uncontrollably …
Knock on my door rips me from my thoughts.
Put down my damn journal, my coffee,
Move my blanket and walk,
One foot then the other to the door,
Where I see a glimpse of your shadow through the blinds.
Turn around, walk back to the couch, sit down,
Cover up with the blanket,
Grab my coffee, grab my journal.
… You have no idea how wrong you are, but how right I wish you were.
Now that is a concept I had not yet pondered:
Sitting here, alone on my couch,
Irritated by you, and yet writing about how I want it to all go away.
Sip my coffee, cuddle with my blanket, close my eyes, and make it
All go away.

Work

I will not say that it is ok, what was said to me last night.
I expected it; I waited for it;
I prepared myself to deal with your reaction.
I will not be flogged for taking care of me.
The guilt you tried to instill in me was unfair and cruel.
If I forgive you, you will do it again,
I refuse to deal with the cruelty again …
Some day it will be ok; maybe we'll control our downfalls;
For now, all we have is to accept it or walk away.
I can accept it for now, because what we have is real.
But you must know that I cannot deal with
That type of reaction much more.
There are other ways to communicate your anger, mistrust, and doubt.
Let's work on communication
So that this will work.

Wonder Wall

Wonder wall, wonder fall
Sack the mounds of virginity—
Sell a story untold
To the world—climb—but do not fall

Settled in your own unrest—labeled
Unpredictable—fallen short
Of an untold story—
Wonder wall—wonder fall.

Design a wall for me to climb
So that fall I may
Someday fall upon
An untold story

Walk up climb this wall
Invented for your past to perish
Bridges burned can be built again
And your past revisited

However, a wonder wall,
Once wonder falls
Can never be
Revisited.

You're Not Being Good

Emotionally, you are a roller coaster
I keep you around just to stop your engine from dying.
You are capable of getting help—
Jump the track, find the straight road again.
The conductor will flip the switch if you ask him to

I am sorry, but I don't like roller coasters
I have to get off this ride right now
I've been on it long enough to know that I am scared
One day—soon—you will go too fast
And your cart will fly off the tracks
I don't know much, but I know this,
I don't want to be on it when that happens.

Mocking Bird

I am a lonely mocking bird
With nothing to mock—

Wolf

You are a wolf in training
You used to be a sheep
Tired of being bitten
You've changed your skin
Dancing with the pack
Hunting with the top dogs.
You once grazed alone—
Scared, frightened of the group
Pushed into the flock
At the shepherd's command
Running, hiding, from the respect
You knew all along—
You deserved it
That some time ago was you
Lonely shepherd cried aloud
Your patience dry
You slay him, his weakness
Your newfound power
Like an owl in the dark of the night
You hunt your pray
With darkened light …